NAMED A BOOK OF THE YEAR BY THE *OBSERVER*, *INDEPENDENT*, *FINANCIAL TIMES*, *EVENING STANDARD*, *STYLIST*, *GRAZIA*, *ELLE*, *HARPER'S BAZAAR*, *FIVE BOOKS* AND *BURO*

'Olivia Sudjic's powerful novel pulses with the strange, fragmented, apocalyptic rhythms of our uneasy present and uncertain future. Visceral and tender, brutal and unspeakably alive, *Asylum Road* digs into the soft heart of our hard times, into intimacies upended by the anthropocene and pulled taut by omnipresent crisis' Alexandra Kleeman

'If positive reviews from the likes of Avni Doshi and Daisy Johnson don't sway you, Sudjic's unsettling, but nonetheless brilliant prose should' *Buro*, Books to look forward to in 2021

'[A] piercingly clear look at a modern world grappling with immigration and history in post-Brexit Britain, through the prism of a couple on the verge of making life-changing decisions. Exploring otherness and the borders between men and women, nations and families, it's edgy, unsettling and yet incredibly sensitive' *The National*, Anticipated books to look out for this year

'Sudjic singularly conveys a feeling so specific to our time – a feeling only her prose can name, and which the reader will instantly recognize. The unsettled, unsettling atmosphere of this book resonates perfectly with its larger states of migration – to or from one's history, one's nation, one's loved ones; away from or towards one's darkest impulses. Smart, edgy and exacting, *Asylum Road* leaves so much unsaid, and shows us the consequences of that' Caoilinn Hughes

'Chilling' *Elle*, Your 2021 Reading List

'[A] sly, unsettling and supremely accomplished story about a former child refugee from Sarajevo named Anya, whose life in Britain dramatically unravels after she gets engaged in her early thirties' *i paper*

'Bold, astonishing and original. Sudjic explores relationships in post-Brexit Britain with her trademark precision and lyricism' Zeba Talkhani

'An impressive novel; Sudjic's cool affect and sense of detachment provides cover for a growing sense of urgency and alienation' *Five Books*, Notable Novels of Spring 2021

'*Asylum Road* is an exceptionally intelligent, sensitive, and thoughtful novel about 21st century life. With subtlety and control, Sudjic powerfully examines the consequences of Brexit, immigration, and historical trauma. With the energy of a thriller and an emotionally raw finale reminiscent of Elena Ferrante, *Asylum Road* is a very special book indeed' Julianne Pachino

'Writing with the offbeat intensity of Deborah Levy, Sudjic offers a discomforting dissection of one woman's fractured identity. Atmospheric and unflinching, *Asylum Road* reveals how the places we seek refuge can ultimately prove to be as toxic as the traumas we flee' Ruth Gilligan

'A swelter of trauma and neurosis, *Asylum Road* is a thrilling, bruising read. Sudjic's prose scythes through political, sexual and class constructs to expose the cruel and fatuous power plays that can undo us at any moment' Shiromi Pinto

'*Asylum Road* masterfully probes the tensions between the identities we inherit and identities we craft. Sudjic's writing coagulates feelings of anxiety and insecurity into an embodied, wrought and visceral experience. *Asylum Road* is that rare novel that dares to probe at uncomfortable questions without flinching from the unwelcome answers that are revealed' Alex Allison

'Electrifying ... A taut, disquieting story ... In precise, elliptical prose, Sudjic paints a powerful portrait of a psyche damaged by war and family schisms. A meditation on identity and belonging, *Asylum Road* speaks to our unsettled times' *Culture Whisper*

'Olivia's latest novel, *Asylum Road*, is a piercing story of trauma, identity and the notion of borders – between families, nations and that meandering line between control and uncontrol, order and absolute chaos. The prose in *Asylum Road* has a cadence that carries you along with a taut urgency' *TOAST Magazine*

'Weaves the tale of a young woman on the brink of marriage, who is haunted by the trauma of her past in the battle of Sarajevo' *Harper's Bazaar*, 10 Best Books of 2021 So Far

'Disturbing and unsettling, there is much about this novel that will compel you to read on. A taut, compulsive second novel rife with wit from the critically-acclaimed Olivia Sudjic, there is a definite Elena Ferrante influence on this work, but that makes it nothing less than riveting' *The Fountain*

'This is a story about beginnings, endings, and the collapse of time between the two ... Each page thrums with anxiety and insecurity, pushing inexorably towards one final, terrifying journey' *Women & Home*

'[A] powerful and thought-provoking read' *Refinery29*

'It has something of the lightness of Rachel Cusk, but is loaded with the weight of Balkan history which cannot be suppressed … an excellent, suspenseful look at how seeming perfection can hide trauma and, ultimately, dissolution' *Arts Desk*

'The story … is rich in characterisation, the claim of history upon the lives of ordinary people, and the interplay between borders and personal identity. It also has one of the most striking final acts in recent fiction, establishing Sudjic as the leading novelist of her generation' *Tortoise*

'Exceptional … *Asylum Road* is a slick, treacly delight – by turns, blackly comic and heart-shattering' *Lunate*

'Anya's feelings of displacement are visceral and they pervade the prose, making it an entirely uneasy, tense read. The experience of reading *Asylum Road* is not a comfortable one, but it is a telling one … Sudjic has made a significant and fresh contribution with her second novel' *F Word*

'Sudjic's prose is clear, crisp and cool … unforgettable' *CultureFly*

'A beautiful novel of borders physical, historical and psychological' *New European*

'Intricately written, this is a brief but intense read' *The Glossary*

'The novel's strength is the beauty of the prose and the prickle of its metaphors' *Elephant Art*

'Sudjic's writing has never been better' *Head Stuff*

'In the restrained, dread-inducing prose of *Asylum Road*, Sudjic has eliminated everything superfluous. Sudjic uses this to make the narrative feel claustrophobic – there's no escape from Anya's anxious mind' *Safe and Sound*

'Stunning … beautifully written and deeply unsettling' *Bookseller*, Editor's Choice

OLIVIA SUDJIC is a writer living in London. She is the author of *Sympathy*, her 2017 debut novel which was a finalist for the Salerno European Book Award and the Collyer Bristow Prize, and *Exposure*, a non-fiction work on anxiety named an *Irish Times*, *Evening Standard* and *White Review* Book of the Year for 2018. Her writing has appeared in publications including the *New York Times*, *Paris Review*, *Financial Times*, *frieze*, *Guardian* and *Granta*.

ALSO BY OLIVIA SUDJIC

Fiction
Sympathy

Non-fiction
Exposure

OLIVIA SUDJIC

ASYLUM ROAD

BLOOMSBURY PUBLISHING
LONDON • OXFORD • NEW YORK • NEW DELHI • SYDNEY

BLOOMSBURY PUBLISHING
Bloomsbury Publishing Plc
50 Bedford Square, London, WC1B 3DP, UK
29 Earlsfort Terrace, Dublin 2, Ireland

BLOOMSBURY, BLOOMSBURY PUBLISHING and the Diana logo
are trademarks of Bloomsbury Publishing Plc

First published in Great Britain 2021
This edition published 2022

A catalogue record for this book is available from the British Library

ISBN: HB: 978-1-5266-1738-5; TPB: 978-1-5266-1739-2;
EBOOK: 978-1-5266-1741-5; EPDF: 978-1-5266-4494-7; PB: 978-1-5266-1740-8

2 4 6 8 10 9 7 5 3 1

Typeset by Integra Software Services Pvt. Ltd.
Printed and bound in Great Britain by CPI Group (UK) Ltd, Croydon CR0 4YY

For Miša and Seja

Between the fear that something would happen and the hope that still it wouldn't, there is much more space than one thinks.

Ivo Andrić

A specter is haunting Western culture – the specter of the Balkans.

Maria Todorova

MOUSEHOLE

I

Sometimes it felt like the murders kept us together.

I'd suggested taking a break, which turned into the holiday, to remedy our real problems – but I knew we'd need one more for the road. They distracted me from my thoughts, from his silences. Murders and holidays were a quick fix that worked.

We drove through London as another body disintegrated, reaching the tunnel at dawn.

Maybe it was ghoulish, my fixation with true crime, but I hate tunnels, and being underground, and the channel one is fifty kilometres.

He knew that about me almost from the start. On our first proper date I went to meet him at the Olympic Stadium. It was 2012. He had tickets for the opening ceremony. Since moving to London I'd avoided the tube and it was July then so I walked, following my phone north across the river, a route which turned out not to be a bridge. That tunnel was designed to curve so you can't see light at the end – so horses wouldn't bolt. As the ceremony began he asked if I wanted his sweater, he could see how badly I was shivering.

Inside the tunnel, the episode ended. We got out, ignoring signs to remain in our vehicle, into the throat that had swallowed us beneath the waves. There was a loud rumbling, but it didn't feel as if we were moving in any particular direction.

Luke hunched over, then pushed his chest out several times. Something cracked. He was stiff already and we hadn't reached France. The complaint was directed at me because I couldn't share the task of driving. I said nothing, showing him alleviating stretches, manipulating him with my hands. The people in the car behind seemed to be staring at us. I felt Luke constrict as he became aware. Maybe they were listening to something as well, I reasoned, their intense concentration focused elsewhere. But I felt paranoid, post-homicide, and we shut ourselves back in the car.

When're you going to learn again? I mean actually take the test.

I sighed and shut my eyes.

I'll pay for it this time. Start when you've got the thesis done.

It was him behind the wheel and I did not have a licence, true, but it was really me who was actually driving. I remember being set on happy-ever-after. It amuses me now, how I thought about it as a physical place at the end of a long road. A place where I could unpack, lie down and never have to move again, and the future became an ending.

Eventually everything stopped, quietened, the car rolled forward a little. We drove out into pale sunshine, a sparse landscape, exposed. He grimaced and tapped the visor down but the brightness came from the road. A shining white fence rose on one side of us and, along it, dust from the ground, or mist. A delicate velvet sheen hovered just above the muddy fields as the sun spread out and silhouetted grey factories. It was peaceful after the tunnel, quiet but for the gentle drone of articulated lorries far-off. Little lakes flashing with white birds. Allotments. A few glinting skylights in the attics of strange homes.

The holiday had begun. I would be on my best behaviour from now on.

I looked over to see what kind of mood he was in.

Luke avoided short-haul flights for environmental reasons. He said he preferred scenic drives. So far, the view was emptiness. The occasional wind turbine standing still, little metal boxes moving up and down the belts of asphalt.

We stopped for coffee at a service station. I waited in the car, staring at a lay-by for HGVs, watching their drivers get out to piss or smoke, remembering the man who'd abandoned a truck crammed with people and left them trapped in there to decompose by the road. A pink rosette of what looked like ham printed on the side, a mysterious beige sauce, a grey lock on the outside of the doors.

Moving again, I opened the window, let the headwinds pummel my cheek. In front of us a truck swerved across the road. Luke shook his head, then slowly, deliberately, switched lanes.

Without knowing the rules of the road, his driving always struck me as exemplary. With other drivers I felt nervous as a passenger, a hand on the door keeping me in but also so I could be ready to jump out. With him I did that very rarely, and then only when another car came too close. He was confident but never reckless. Driving, at least, he never gave me any reason to doubt his ability to read the intentions of others or communicate his own.

Now I concentrated on the gentle incline on one side. When it thinned, or the road rose, I concentrated on the endless brown fields beyond, the outlines of slender trees in rows.

OK Loris? You're very quiet.

I nodded.

Carsick?

Loris was one in a series of names. The cute primate, which at one time colonised parts of the internet, clutching a tiny umbrella or stretching their arms into the air. The people who buy these creatures illegally don't realise the saliva is poisonous. Even with their tiny teeth removed, the venom can be deadly.

We passed names on the map that made me think back to school exams. The mist disappeared. I could make out steeply pitched roofs – pitched, he said, for snow.

They'll get flatter as we go south. South of Lyon the climate changes.

I admired how he knew these things. These invisible rules of the land, like the road. Or not quite like the road because they were innate.

My skin felt greasy and I closed the window. The silence between us grew. I resisted the impulse to play another true crime episode and rubbed my hand beneath my chin. We passed memorials and where Charles de Gaulle had lived, my fingernail grazing back and forth along my jaw.

Luke rarely commented on this now, but initially he'd compared the habit to stereotypic behaviour. I'd thought this meant stereotypical but in fact it's a kind of death drive:

> The mysterious, repetitive range of actions displayed by captive animals such as pacing, picking without

purpose, and even self-harm, indicative of psychological distress in artificial environments since it is not observed in animals in the wild.

I never said what I was actually doing, which was feeling for the sharp hairs that surfaced there. An insurrectionary beard I was always monitoring. I forced myself to stop now and examined my hands. My knuckles would need shaving.

I knew other women who'd given up that unwinnable war with their bodies, even the jawline razor wire, but I'd now concealed my natural state so long, why spoil things when I'd succeeded?

Of the things I cared too much about then, one was appearing civilised. In ethical terms but also in aesthetic ones. I had read the right books, bought thrifted designer clothes, gained several degrees at elite institutions and, in Luke's flat, arranged an elegant mise-en-scène that in fact held no emotional resonance. They were props, these objects I combed from life, smooth pebbles that had once been cliffs.

I love that first bit out of a toll station, unmarked, where you can move away on clean road. Those were the times it seemed to me I might like to drive myself.

*

We reached our stopover in the afternoon and eventually found the hotel. The small dining room was all couples, none of whom spoke much. Cutlery on china, teeth on glass – I saw Luke going inward to escape it. He said he was too tired for more than one course, leaving before I'd finished.

When I came back to the room, minutes after, it was pitch-black and I could hear him breathing. I moved toward the bed, tapping the mattress in the dark, and climbed, in facing away. A few minutes passed before he turned, curled round, and, after momentary resistance, I hooked my foot behind his knee.

I waited for his hands to find me, but gradually his body lost tension until he jerked. I turned over – his dark shape like a hill faraway.

My phone said it was midnight, which meant it was our anniversary. On the first one I remembered feeling warm, insulated from the outside world. The second, I kept sensing what I thought was a phantom draught. The third I saw a detailed map of hairline cracks spreading out across the table between us. I did not mark our fourth but waited to see if he would. He did not. Today was our fifth. I'd reminded him when we booked the holiday.

Christopher said it was a natural response to capitalism, these tensions in what he disparagingly called monogamous, cishet relationships – particularly my sense that sex was a job, and not doing it the one way I could hold power.

He often referred to a friend who lived in a commune. They seemed to have a lot of sex. Feeling square, anxious just thinking about it, I reminded him my parents were communists. But it was true that nostalgia had replaced hope. When we did have sex now it was usually followed by a feeling of dissolution that seemed more intense than normal post-sex loneliness, at least for me. Solving a murder was a better way for us to feel connected.

I woke up and knew he was gone before I saw it. I listened for sounds in the bathroom and tried to remember whether we'd had an argument at some point in the night.

Our arguments were mostly silent, or silent on his side. Often in the dark, lying in bed so neither face could see the other. Not an argument then, but a pressure. A malignant quiet that sank into the mattress until I couldn't bear to lie there. I would get up in a dramatic fashion, go down to the sofa, then crawl back in a few hours later when he was sound asleep. Once he'd left for work in the morning, an email would usually arrive with a link he knew I'd like, and it was as if the night's events had been the product of my imagination.

He would have gone running, I told myself as I lay in the hotel bed. There was a path along the perimeter of the hotel grounds that cut through woods. Someone had tied colour-coded ribbons onto branches to mark two routes. Blue led you in a circle round the property, green took you on another path out of the grounds. We'd walked the blue route together soon after arriving the previous evening, ending where we began after half an hour or so. He'd said then he might wake early to do it.

I told myself I had no reason to feel rejected, dressed, then went back to the same table we'd eaten at.

I put my book down, split open, and watched as the other guests began to notice me. Last night's wine had sedimented in my lower lip and without thinking I peeled away a strip. I could taste the sourness of my own blood, pulsing.

After a while I realised breakfast was self-service. Standing by the buffet table, I held a napkin to my lip and made a show of examining the pastries wrapped in heavy cloth. I cut a slice of breakfast cake with slow precision. The other tables emptied and I became more self-conscious. The blood was still blooming into the napkin. I could not touch my food, except to cut it into smaller and smaller pieces, as if I were the kind of lonely, hungry woman liable to choke while eating. When I couldn't cut anything in two again, I left the knife at an inconclusive angle, as if to say I was still considering what I might do with it.

Two maids began clearing. I finished my glass of cold green tea and got up with what I hoped looked like nonchalance, as if Luke was never supposed to join me. I held the book to my chest, feeling my heart begin to thud against it, and went back to our room.

Not there.

I opened the shutters, looking around as if I'd lost an inanimate object that could not reveal itself. The sun was high, bars of it crossed the floor. The bedcovers were still thrown back on his side, his boxers and shirt on the floor where he'd shed them.

It was habit to think of crime scenes. I told myself to concentrate, looking around slowly and noting his phone, dead on the bedside table. The table was actually a bookcase of warped paperbacks and crisp hardbacks never read. My eyes rested on a title about survival. I drew it out. On closer inspection, a survival A–Z. The novelty kind with illustrations. I'd owned something like it as a child, or perhaps even the same one. Dangers were illustrated in a way that felt calming, like the sedate line drawings of airline safety manuals. I'd remembered one instruction, in particular, that if you fell down a waterfall you were supposed to close your legs to prevent internal rupturing.

I looked at the dust jacket with the uncanny sense it was my own copy transplanted here. The spine cracked as I opened it. Quicksand. The trick with that I knew already. Lie very still and flat.

> On no account struggle or attempt to pull yourself out.

I plugged his phone in, switched to my canvas shoes, then went to find the pool, hoping I would see him swimming or reading. The sun was hot as I marched along the passage that led away from the main building, shielding my phone to check the time.

At the pool I swore under my breath and circled the loungers. No sign. I stood over my reflection at the deep end. A dead scorpion swayed on the bottom. I told myself this was not a sign of anything. I was reading into things again. This was simply absence. Absence with an absence of meaning.

I went back to reception. The same woman who'd cleared the breakfast and observed my solitude. I asked her in French for a bottle of water and she extracted one, unsmiling. I bared my teeth gratefully as she handed it over. She checked my room number, wrote it down, then went back to a game she had been playing on her phone.

*

I stood in the shade of the front gates and watched time creep closer to something categorically wrong. He knew how I hated to be left, with or without warning, but would've decided to forget how this went. He liked to assert his freedom by doing it I guessed. While he was gone I'd go through all the best-case scenarios, pacing like someone under house arrest. The narrative becoming ever more complicated. By the time he returned I'd be hysterical, then livid, then contrite. I would find myself apologising to him, neck bent, applying pressure to some part of him, begging forgiveness for my offence.

Our walk the previous evening had taken maximum forty minutes at a slow pace. I hesitated at the other external gate that marked the start of both routes – the simple choice now fraught – before embarking on the blue. I would retrace my steps. I would find him reclining somewhere along the path in the shade. And if not, he would have taken the green route into town and settled somewhere picturesque. I imagined a large white umbrella in a concrete stand and a glass ashtray into which he would have deposited wet olive stones. The same light that had suffused my vision of this trip. He would greet me with a bemused expression, to remind me I did not own him.

The wood was dense and the way obscured by branches. Alone, I had to focus harder on following the route. The path was sandy and my calves began to burn. I could feel blisters rising behind my heels and sweat prickling beneath the hair against my neck. Occasionally something Luke-sized would appear – the reptilian markings of a shoe – but these would slip away into sandy crests which went off in all directions.

It seemed safe to assume no other guests would be walking in the heat and that it would be possible now to shout his name. It was an ostentatious thing to do. If he was nearby and could hear me, I would feel humiliated. The silence, on the other hand, felt oppressive. I tried it out but couldn't raise my voice above a whisper. I stood still, panting, trying to summon something louder. Sweat crept into my eyes. The heavy glass bottle was now empty, sliding in my hands. No sound.

In the distance then, a bell. I strained, trying to decide if it was coming from ahead or behind, moving back and then forward again, then running, steps erratic on the sand. The bell grew louder and at the next turn, the trees thinned. I stopped, my throat thick with dust and saliva I couldn't swallow. A dozen horses stood in front of me in a clearing, tossing their heads in the shade. The bell hung from the neck of the most magnificent. It rang each time the horse moved its head or passed the heavy air through its nose.

I sank to my knees, heart at my temples. I knelt in that pose as a child, waiting for absent people.

From kneeling I soon lay down, thinking not of happy endings to this situation, but what it would be like to hear the worst. The horses snorted and kicked the air, perturbed. My nose stung, as if I was about to start crying, but then, as the minutes passed, the pain faded. It began to seem like another thing I might survive and my breathing slowed again.

I grew quiet, save the occasional gasp, and eventually very still, feeling the heat of the earth against my back, staring at the branches swaying. From survivable it became tolerable. And from tolerable, gradually, something else. My heart soothed inside my ribs. I felt a kind of unity with my surroundings. The old trees, the rocks that had endured. The horses grew accustomed to my presence, and I with them, until I realised the worst now felt desirable, like release.

2

After my brother died, my father said a suicide could be hard to detect because the person, having decided on death, has accepted the worst and may feel more at peace. They might seem happy even, the struggle and indecision lifted, an end to the tunnel near.

But when Luke returned from his solo excursion he was agitated, packing without meeting my eyes, paying the bill in a hurry, then driving us further south for hours in almost total silence. I decided he was not suicidal, he had simply wanted a morning alone to see the town, but I felt my body brace, like the drawing of the woman before the waterfall, everything sealed to protect against the rupture.

When I told the story of what happened after, I described the golden-hour heat and the view. Us seated on a balcony overlooking a small fishing port. A still pool shaded by umbrella pines. I didn't say I thought he was about to break up with me.

Anya, he said.

The cicadas seemed to intensify. All at once their separate mating calls surged as one siren song. A rasping sound that rose from everything on earth. He took my phone from my hand and set it aside, began to speak of a fork in the road. Something rose in my throat, hard and tight, I put my hand to it and hid by pressing into him, feeling our separate heartbeats hammer away in mutual dread. He released himself, got up. I thought he was leaving me but then he knelt. He lifted his hands, offering me a box.

The yellow diamond flared green and white. On my finger, I could see it even out of the corner of my eye – an aurora that followed me everywhere.

It had been his grandmother's. Now, he said, sounding unconvinced, it would be mine.

We stayed to watch the light bleed out. Somewhere an insect beat relentlessly against a screen and the sky turned a pink so saccharine my teeth began to ache.

I stopped sleeping. Luke's sleep changed too, which I knew because I only slept intermittently by day beside the pool. At night I watched him. I told myself the cause of my insomnia was the heat and mosquito hordes. The mattress was too hard. I watched the retreating tail of the green repellent coil, the hours burning off.

He'd look angry in his dreams. He'd twitch then make a startled noise and lurch upright, hot and damp

– What? he'd shout, like I'd shoved him. What're you doing to me?

In the mornings he'd rise stealthily and go running. I'd pretend to be asleep.

When he came back I'd be waiting. I'd watch him through one eye as he undressed. Waiting again while he took a shower, watching again while he dried off. His penis pale beside his darkening legs. It started to look sickly. If he caught me with my eyes open, I turned my gaze to the yellow diamond, turning it slowly and deliberately so that it would catch the light.

I'd taken several books by Sybille Bedford with me on that holiday. Every place, person and meal she described sounded like a secret language of sophistication. I read them in the sun by the pool while Luke read his apocalypse books in the shade, their titles all in sans serif. I found myself wishing to be like her. Bedford. Hedonistic. Denying my own hunger for security.

One of the books Luke read revived his idea of getting a communal smallholding and living off the land. I wondered why he'd suggested getting married if society would soon collapse but I didn't ask out loud. Not just because Luke talked about environmental issues in increasingly technical terms, as if irritated his pet cause had grown popular, but because the subject of our engagement quickly felt too awkward to return to.

When I thought about it I felt a peculiar foreboding. It was not the feeling I'd expected when I imagined this initiation into married life. Though we inhabited the same villa and had nothing else to talk about, we barely spoke of it again. Without the ring, I'd have convinced myself I'd imagined it.

I reasoned that this was probably for the best. I did not want a white wedding or the associated rituals. Weddings seem like hubris and perhaps they invite disaster. But I wanted the institution of marriage. To change my surname to Luke's and be shielded by it. Bedford had become Bedford by one of those strategic marriages that happened between Jews and gays in the 1930s.

Most people we knew were married by then. Christopher said it was reactionary. Luke and I owed our first meeting to the wedding of our only mutual friends, and since then I'd paid attention to ring-fingers, to the self-confidence of these women, like expensive cats that had all been microchipped. My ringless finger marked me as a stray among them. Something pitiable and out of place, which made me want it more, not just for protection but as validation. By that summer, listening to tales of yet another engagement could produce strange reactions in me. I'd ask the newly affianced if she'd been uneasy, following her suspicious-acting partner out onto some remote cliff face like that. A rock to the head instead of the hand! Only I would laugh at this.

I laughed louder just to cover Luke's unnerving silence, but there was resentment I could barely hide. A cold part at the very centre of me, painful, as if my underwire had pierced my flesh. My smile would droop on one side. What's wrong? he sometimes asked as we left the creamy folds of another marquee. You look like you've got Bell's palsy. My feet would hurt from being bound in foolish shoes. I'd run a bath in yet another B&B, soap my arms and slide the razor, going carefully round each wrist.

Now I had a ring of my own. This was what I'd wanted. This was where everything in my life had led. This rented villa in the South of France. This man beside this pool. Occasionally dozing or plunging into the freezing water. But the longing was still there. I stared at the ring to remind myself of my new status, and, fresh from a dive, the breeze cold on my skin, the sun warming it, the view beyond the trees could then suggest something infinite, some new place I now had access to.

The last Bedford book I read was her travel essays. One describes her drive across the Italian border and then through Yugoslavia. She is driving slowly, in a sturdier car than her own, rented so as to be expendable, apprehensive not only regarding the roads but of entering a socialist federalist republic where *their* idea of freedom is not the same as *ours*. Where 'communism is the price for peace'. She describes the road to Split along the Dalmatian coast – the mountains, the green of the sea, the mist like a bloom on a peach – as the most wonderful drive she had ever experienced.

When we returned to London, Big Ben had been stopped, and scaffolding now obscured the clock tower alongside parts of the Houses of Parliament. When I pointed this out as we drove past, Luke said that given the current situation the symbolism was too crude to mention, as if this was what I'd said.

We dropped the car at home then went straight out again to an Italian restaurant where his friends congratulated us. We had them back to the flat and the toasts continued with wine Luke had brought from France. The women inspected the diamond as if for flaws. My drooping smile returned. Now it was my turn for Mason jars. For personalised vows like annual reviews – helping someone live their values.

I went to bed long after him, having cleaned the kitchen. He had put a crime podcast on and fallen asleep but I lay there listening to it.

The following morning, the sticky remains of a bird could be seen when I stood at the kitchen sink washing the wine glasses that were too large to go in the machine. I'd bought them for his birthday. A stupid purchase I could not afford. It seemed too high for a cat to reach the slate roof which jutted out from the back wall, so how, I wondered, had it got there?

He came in as I was drying them and told me his parents had invited us to Cornwall. He'd go that afternoon and make the most of the holiday he still had left to take, I could join them on the weekend.

They had known what Luke was planning to do in France. His mother had provided the ring. It was unclear what remained to be discussed privately between them, but I agreed to stay behind.

September was ending but the temperature reached a sinister twenty-nine degrees. Every day was meant to cede to storms. I waited for rain to wash the tiles of the bird remains. The city heat made my insomnia worse. Finally I gave in and bought an expensive fan. Once I'd carried it home the heatwave ended – and it rained non-stop for days.

The noise of the downpour helped me sleep, and in sleep it also entered my dreams. The sea levels had risen so that half of the British Isles were flooded. Luke directed me by text to meet him at a safe place but I had to sort out something first with my family. Once this was done, I could no longer find the message with Luke's instructions, and the water meant I could no longer find my way back to the flat as all landmarks had been submerged.

When I woke I texted Luke to tell him, even though he has no interest in these things. His reply came slowly but was comforting:

I'm sorry. It's hard to get back to places in dreams.

On Friday I walked most of the way in the rain to the station, relishing the new smell of the earth.

I meant to work on the train but spent the hours watching the landscape change. I'd requested forward-facing with a table but was given a rearward seat. This happened every time I took the train to Penzance. I suppose they rarely know which way carriages will be facing when they allocate seats, but somehow it felt personal.

I could have switched – there were empty forward-facing seats – but I hated doing this. I couldn't stand the tension when the train arrived at each station and new passengers got on, their eyes boring into me as they moved along the aisle. And I couldn't bear the shame of being told to move if I'd taken a place that did not belong to me.

This paranoia was most acute on the way to see his parents, perhaps because of everything I knew from Luke about the native Cornish view of outsiders, or 'emmets' as he called them. His own mother had moved there as a child but made up for it with Cornish nationalism and loud suspicion of second-homers, which her own parents had once been.

The journey to Mousehole was by then familiar. There were stretches of scenery I knew to look out for. I liked the thunk thunk of the doors and the whistle each time we pulled away, ever closer until I could recite the stations. They have good place names in that part of the world, easy to romanticise. Like in Scotland, they get wilder as you approach extremity. I liked to imagine the submarine cables emerging onto the rocks at Porthcurno, connecting this island to the world. It made my skin prick – something about the inevitability of the tracks, taking me as far as they could before land fell into sea.

The man sitting opposite, where I'd wanted to sit, wore a Help for Heroes hoodie, unzipped to reveal an England football shirt. I glanced under the table to see a hybrid of hiking boots and trainers, a gold signet ring, a gold wedding band on the other hand resting on his thigh, a silver dog-tag-style bracelet hanging from his sleeve, a red poppy keychain fastened to his rucksack. He had the shining, ruddy skin of a younger man, his grey hair shorn in a military style. I looked into his eyes for a moment – large and black with no discernible irises. He reached down into his bag, pulling out the same flask Luke had, drinking from it then folding his arms, staring directly back at me.

I wondered now if I had the wrong seat after all. No. I knew I was being paranoid again. I switched my gaze to the window. A wide brown expanse slanted with boats at low tide. The view for that part of the journey is how I imagine Doggerland.

Occasionally I caught the eye of the woman at the opposite table, which she shared with two children and a man. I guessed from the proximity of their legs that they were her children and he was her husband, but in the five hours until they alighted at St Austell, I never saw one of them look up from their screen. She was conspicuous for not having anything to occupy her attention and her pale skin seemed to be lit by a different source, belonging neither to the train nor any of the worlds in which her family were separately engrossed.

When our gaze met at Dawlish as the train grazed the sea, I sensed something strange in my vision. The speed of the train seemed to accelerate, dizzyingly, like we might reach the horizon. Looking at her, it was as if either she or I weren't really there but regarding the other from another point in time.

Later, as I stood between carriages in preparation for my stop – the last – I remember thinking: I'll be alright if he breaks this off because I'll still have the PhD to finish. I'll crawl deeper into that black hole. The more dependable institution. The hammering in my heart again, the war drum starting up.

*

He was waiting beyond the railings. He wore an unfamiliar coat. I didn't recognise him until he got out and signalled from the door of his dad's car. The sticker in the window – Kernow, with the white cross on black. Even then I saw him as a stranger. This was a phenomenon I recognised when we spent time apart, but the physical attraction now took me by surprise.

His mother often said Luke had been a late bloomer. He'd been substantial as a child. Durable, like the white goods that come with five-year guarantees. You could see the evolution in her framed photographs – which were everywhere – how he'd whittled into his present form, head separating out from neck. Lately his newfound fanaticism for running had made him sinewy.

I dropped my bag and held out my arms to what was left of him. The yellow diamond flared. Luke kissed the top of my head and pressed me into the thick, fan-shaped muscle of his chest. I reached inside the strange oilskin then withdrew, holding him at arm's length. He had the beginnings of a beard.

Hello . . . ? I touched his face and then the coat.

It's Dad's.

I felt him take in my appearance now, worrying I'd applied too much foundation. He hated make-up, and then when he commented on it, I'd feel the self-conscious urge to wear more.

I felt nervous, I said, on the way here.

Me too.

Driving down or coming to pick me up?

He took my bag but did not answer.

How are they?

Fine.

Listing Luke's good traits, filial duty went near the top, but I'd never felt closer to him than during the previous summer, when he and his parents had fallen out. They had said it would be *suicide* staying in Europe, while Luke thought that word would be more apt if we left. Sorry, he said after, I only meant –

I assured him I didn't mind. Being taken into his confidence, listening to him rage behind their back, had produced a mirage of married life which lasted the duration of the rift. From the referendum until his mother called to check we were still alive when concrete barriers were installed on London's major bridges.

All arguments about sovereignty were suspended after those attacks. They asked if he wanted to move back. Now he minimised their estrangement, and seemed to resent me for what I remembered. I couldn't understand what had gone on between them, he insisted.

I'm sure his parents thought that I had been the cause of it. The cosmopolitanism I'd tried so hard to cultivate did not succeed at charming them. We had a row about it, maybe the closest Luke and I ever got to a real fight. He characterised his parents' aversion to the bloc with ever more left-wing arguments, which I could not dispute although it was maddening. If I ever mentioned the conspiracy theories she bought into now, he leapt to her defence. If her trust in institutions was disintegrating, he said, it was even more important to hold her close. I knew that this was his way of reconciling his parents with his own world view. It was commendable, in a way, how he, a scientist, modified these facts out of loyalty. He'd been doing this ever since he went to university it seemed. Despite what Luke did for a job, his mother did not believe the world was warming, and her resistance had only grown alongside her son's expertise. I'd wondered if it was a reaction to it, as if she had to compete with science, but actually it had started long before. She had refused all vaccinations for him growing up. The way she'd told me this, proprietorially, made it clear his body would never belong to me.

I climbed onto the passenger seat, held up my newspaper, its front page still on fire:

NEW DEATH TRAPS FOUND

Good to get out, I said.

He glanced at the photograph.

Of the city, I mean.

OK, how are you?

I realised my error – talking about Cornwall as an escape irritated him.

Fine.

He claimed to have poor reception when he went home. He called it home though he also used that word for our flat. His flat. The flat his parents bought. Whenever he went to Mousehole, I expected minimal contact, so that when we were reunited, there was usually a period of adjustment, of having to make small talk as strangers might. Luke inscrutable, me eager and puppyish, sniffing out each interstice.

This separateness could last for hours unless we had news to tell. I thought back over the past week. I'd spent it eating leftover chicken pho, digging through fat which had solidified a greenish grey, leaving the flat only for small intervals of sun or to work in air-conditioned cafes or the British Library, alone. I'd achieved nothing. Several versions of a diagram, the tensile limits of my cables.

When Luke was away I could turn feral on my own. I tried to think of something to tell him as he edged out of the station, but as I opened my mouth he pressed resume. The timbre of the podcaster familiar.

I've done a lot of driving, he said noticing my look. It's different when I'm alone.

OK, can you fill me in?

You'll catch up.

I was sensitive to that tone. I inferred from the tightness in it, like a wire stretched from the wall, that he'd reached his conversational limit during the week and had taken refuge in the solitude of the car before I'd broken it.

I kept my eyes out the window, on the stream of moss-covered roofs, stone walls, dark slate. One of the hosts thought the murderer was not a monster until society had made him one, the other took a more 'Hobbesian' view.

Outside the town, the trees on either side of the road interlaced their branches to make tunnels. The roads became narrow lanes with fields either side of tall hedgerows. Then something one host said made me open my mouth without thinking.

Any infestations I should know about?

He was silent long enough to unnerve me.

Not in the house.

The first time I'd visited, a swarm of bees had exploded from the attic and the bluebell patch his mother cultivated was under threat from badgers – leaving me with serum sickness and the confused impression that badgers went out at night to gather bluebells. I heard Luke refer to me, upstairs, as the convalescent. I wasn't *listening* – I'd been afraid of drifting off in case my mouth fell open. I was terrorised by small creatures. When I caught something scaling the wall, I left it dashed there as a warning until Luke had said there'd be other things that came now because they were *attracted*.

What does that mean, not in the house?

He stopped the podcast, softening. Moles were tunnelling in the front garden, he said. His father had abandoned the roller, conceding the area in the hope they'd be happy there and call it a day.

But moles *like* tunnelling, he went on. It's not a war you can win with them. They swim through the earth. If I was blind I'd do it too. But obviously my mother is losing sleep over it.

Anne hated the idea of losing control of her property, whether to me when I tried to help her with domestic tasks, or to the moles, the crowning glory being the lawn at the back which she mowed in stripes sitting on top of a large machine. When she was not mowing she gazed at it from the kitchen window or watched protectively from the door.

Luke had found a vibrating device that claimed to deter moles, believing it was better to use preventative measures rather than combative ones. He suspected his mother still kept a supply of strychnine, despite it being banned.

Outside the breeding season, he continued, moles live alone and defend their tunnels aggressively. Maybe several will inhabit the same area, but each makes a separate system. She goes after them when she's mowing but they burrow right down and instead she kills everything else in her path. Frogs and voles get spattered everywhere. I've convinced her to let me use a scythe for the long grass, that way they have a chance to escape.

He began telling me about his rewilding plans to convert one part of the garden into a meadow, and I stopped following him.

Some of the times I felt most sure of Luke involved watching him free wild animals. In France he'd saved a small green frog from the bath by throwing a wet cloth over it and carrying it outside. The frog kept coming back. It did not want to exist in a state of nature, preferring the cool sarcophagus of the bath despite our looming presence over him. Maybe, I suggested, it felt safer there from other predators.

Around the time I moved into his flat, a bird fell down the chimney and beat against the window. Luke guided it down to waist height with the soft end of a broom. I stood dumbly by, conscious my ovaries were pulsing. When I couldn't turn the window locks, he made me take the bird. I was afraid to touch it, and the fear only intensified when I did, the throb of tiny life, the crush of feathers ossified inside my hands. I didn't mention my father's nets, hung in trees so we could catch birds like it to eat.

He punched the horn in warning as we approached a bend.

When we started seeing each other, I'd asked him just to drive me around. He said I was likely the only person aroused by authority in the form of the highway code. I'd made a joke (auto-eroticism) but he'd looked blank. Now I imagined him driving other girls for whom the car itself was the fetish. I saw him going faster along these lanes, someone's sandy foot, toe ring on leather, blonde hair furious in the wind.

Did you ever surf? I asked suddenly, interrupting him.

He paused, narrowing his eyes. Why?

No reason.

We'd once pulled into a disused quarry somewhere not far from where we were, and I'd tried to persuade him to fuck me against the car. In the end he let me go down on him. It was the first time he'd allowed this and I remember his visible shock when I swallowed the mouthful like seawater. I'd sensed that I'd misjudged him, or misunderstood something much greater about that act. Before we met I'd always been looking to please this way. Confusing the desire to please with my own pleasure. But as we drove out of the quarry, I saw him revising his understanding of who I was also, and felt as if something solid beneath me had given way.

As we got closer to his parents', the cat's eyes began to shine from the road, the headlights making a pale wreath ahead of us, illuminating the side of a cottage daubed with the words ENGLISH OUT.

We passed the church where Luke's parents got married, which I knew would be the theme of our weekend. Then, at the end of the tarmac, I touched his hand. I had the feeling, close to homesickness, of longing to be there even though I was. Finally, the garden wall covered in lichen, the barking of the dog.

As a child I'd fantasised about a low-beamed, thatch-roofed cottage from British children's books, and no matter how many times I arrived, it still felt like stepping inside that fantasy.

We entered the hall as, from the back garden, Anne came in, carrying a torch and covered in dirt. Her grey hair had turned white in the sun. She gestured to her smock and gardening gloves, then walked toward the sink with her hands up as if I held a gun.

Michael appeared behind her. He had to stoop, and from this posture, the tic of rolling his shoulders and his beak of a nose, I'd always associated him with a large bird. More blood vessels had broken across his face, darkest on the chin where white tufts of hair also sprouted. When he leant toward me I saw the deep folds of skin that intersected at his neck. His scalp was mottled brown. I tried to imagine Luke at that age.

Train OK?

Fine, thanks.

Luke got you OK?

Yes.

Given that we were both standing there, I wondered if this question was meant to draw attention to the fact I was reliant on him to drive me, as well as everything else.

Oh I nearly forgot. Congratulations!

Well, he corrected himself, it's Luke who is lucky.

I appreciated this. Any indication they did not view me as a parasite, looking for a fold in their family. I made that sound that is laughter without smiling and placed the hand with the ring on Luke's chest, leaning into his shoulder in a way that was supposed to be a parody. It had made his friends laugh but Michael only nodded.

Upstairs, I unpacked and Luke sat on the bed, leaning back on his elbows. A book had been left at an angle on the desk. I turned it over. A volume of poetry by a Cornish poet. This was Anne's mode of diplomacy. Not poetry as such, but objects she thought I'd like left out without explanation.

Luke pulled me onto the bed. The distant look was gone. He climbed over me and I smiled. I felt powerful and steady and stopped his hands in their tracks.

We should help your mum.

He froze for a moment, then groaned, pushed his erection against his stomach with his waistband.

Anne gave me a pile of new napkins to put out instead of the ones I'd used to set the table. They were decorated with little blue pictures and accompanying Cornish nouns.

There's a picture in their downstairs toilet, a framed photo of their whole extended family, all smiles except Michael, mid-soliloquy. They're standing by the monument to Dorothy Pentreath – supposedly the last person who conversed in that language.

When the table was done, Anne gave us beans to shell. My way was to split their seams gently and slide them along, Luke's was to snap the pod in the middle and press, so they shot out like bullets, ringing against the pan.

Anne stood at the sink peeling potatoes until I noted a small yellow fly on Luke's shirt and she spun round, pointing the peeler at me.

There were so many bloody apricots over the summer I had to make buckets of jam. And then the flies came. They were *out* of control. I had to make a trap – she indicated the counter where a glass bowl was filled with liquid – using vinegar. Not as good as the sticky paper but we ran out. Chaos. I tell you now, I nearly lost my mind.

She flushed, pinged the elastic of her neckline and blew back her white fringe. Luke bent over the bowl, wrinkling his nose, and I came closer too, thinking of bleeding apricots. Some flies had drowned but many more sat on the rim, watching their friends sink into amber. There was something languid about the scene, like the aftermath of a wild party.

The first meal I had in that house I realised that the plates we were eating off were the exact same as my aunt's when I lived with her in Glasgow. In Glasgow, I'd felt the same sensation, seeing that my aunt had the same lace crochet table runner as my mother – an uncanny effect of making me feel less at home. Every time I sat down to a meal Anne had made, I had the urge to comment on them. I stopped myself. Other than being dull, I worried it sounded like I was trying to prove something.

Anne took her seat finally and said, Well. She wanted to discuss our wedding. I tried not to look at her crowded little mouth. Full of overlapping teeth like a shark. A bone from the fish pie stuck in my throat, scratching it, so that I kept trying to clear it even after it was gone. Each time I did, everyone would stop talking and look at me expectantly and I would have to wave the conversation on. Luke seemed reluctant to engage so his mother couldn't get very far with her questioning.

Here, Anne said as I cleared my throat again, eat some bread.

Michael changed the subject to their hostilities with some neighbours. Second-homers who'd complained that the trees in Luke's parents' garden obscured their view.

A petition was sent. Anne didn't recognise *any* of the names. Now two trees had fallen within weeks of each other, though there'd hardly been a breeze.

They know we know they poisoned them, she said. I suppose we're lucky they fell toward the road. But there might be more any day now. Or as we sleep. We could all be killed. I've asked Paul to have a look.

Until the first – and only – time I saw his parents in London, I'd thought they had no fears. Then Anne said she had heard my university was a hotbed of terrorism and she seemed eroded, standing there in our kitchen.

She had once been in the news, I remembered as we cleared the table, with the headline BRAVE LOCAL WOMAN SURVIVES COLLAPSE. While walking the dog along a cliff she'd spotted something strange – the land moving – and filmed the moment when a section of cliff collapsed onto the beach. In the interview with a local reporter she says that the sea, which had always seemed to her like a defensive moat, had threatened to eat her up. I searched for it again. There were now links to other reports about sea defences, a story of a man in Southwold who was fighting both nature and bureaucracy at once, and a scientific study which claimed Cornwall had at one time formed part of France, owing to a clear geological boundary.

*

After dinner we sat in front of a documentary. A penguin couple arched their necks in a synchronised, hypnotic dance. The ritual helped the pair to bond, the voice-over explained. Luke, lips dark with wine, provided meta-narration based on the extent to which the programme anthropomorphised its subjects.

I liked the superimposed narratives. The animals wanted the same things I did. We learned that puffins die at thirty, have one offspring at a time, and mate for life.

I don't believe it, Luke said, they must get divorced.

But even he was transfixed by the bowerbird. Michael liked the way it could shrink and expand its pupils to seduce. Anne admired its thatch of orchid stems and neatly planted lawn. Luke said the way the bird accumulated and displayed treasures in its theatre reminded him of someone, meaning me.

What's the opposite of anthropomorphise? I said.

Dehumanise, Michael said, unaware, again, I'd made a joke.

Zoomorphism, Luke corrected.

I'd watched a lot of TV the summer my sister and I arrived in the UK. I sat indoors with the curtains drawn watching Home Front when it was still hosted by Tessa Shaw. After that came Changing Rooms, Better Homes, Grand Designs. We hadn't been able to watch TV for months at a time so my aunt allowed it at first.

It was perhaps the easiest way to deal with me. Then she let it go on as it became clear I was gaining a precocious vocabulary: *feature walls*, *imitation mahogany*, *local vernacular*.

By the time I started my new school, I felt a primitive desire for accumulation. I lusted after swag curtains and ornaments visible through the windows on more affluent streets. I stole small items from children in my class. The first was a gaudy tassel from the skirt of an armchair which I stored in a shoebox under my bed. It had relieved the tight feeling in my chest for a few days.

After the main programme ended and the bit about how it was made came on, Michael returned to his crossword.

Shibboleth, he barked suddenly. Five letters.

We were silent for a while. All I could think of was Doris Salcedo's crack in the Turbine Hall floor.

I wish they gave clues, I said at last.

His eyebrows jumped and then the three of them burst into laughter. I smiled though I didn't get the joke, then for real as I understood, and then, with a radiating warmth because Anne had put her arm around my shoulder in a clumsy way – a hug, in essence – and I felt as if I'd finally stepped over her threshold. I had a vision of the four of us in the cottage, seen in cross section. Miniature figures, like in a doll's house, moving between scenes. I saw us from the other side of this vertical plane, from where I seemed a part of it.

Upstairs, undressing, I held him off again. Then I lay back to read the poetry book.

The poet was deaf-blind, the foreword said. People wrote on his hand so he could communicate. He was also a self-proclaimed *sex mystic*.

Have your parents read this?

Luke, his face now deep in the pillow, was unresponsive.

I tried to feel my way into the deprivation of those two senses, to step into being deaf-blind like an analgesic suit. I imagined it like a special power of concentration.

The poet wrote about the landscape of china clay mining. I'd seen some of what remained: the scars, the quarries turned lakes. Luke had taken me to the Eden Project – built in reclaimed china clay pits, now home to a transplanted forest. It had been the first time he talked to me in any detail about biodiversity – his field.

I remember first explicitly wanting to marry him that day, moved by how much he seemed to care about future lives. That went on my mental list with filial loyalty and the way he liked to do repairs, or own things that needed constant maintenance. All things which suggested reliability.

I put the book down, turned off the light and lay my head beside his. A rush of warmth spread across the pillow. The bead of water that had rolled into the canals of my ear on the last day of our French holiday had tormented me at first, but by then, two weeks later, it must have travelled to a sanctum so deep inside I'd ceased to feel it. Now it was gone, I felt rehabilitated. I lay on my side, holding him from behind, imagining the day when this house would be ours.

The water cooled beneath my cheek. I could feel the whirr of sleeplessness accelerating. I tried to imagine us living in a simpler time. In the time of china clay mining. I could see myself with an auburn dog and soft-bellied children: blob-like shapes, legs blotted with pink bruises. They ran around and splashed in the craters filled with turbid water.

I did fall asleep but had one of my recurring dreams in which I can't. These are almost exact replicas of the nights in which I lie awake. The night sky is always a saturated yellow, like there will be a storm but there never is. The window is broken, or I can't close it, but there is a metal bowl beneath a drain pipe, catching rainwater for someone to drink. The drips ring out, unpredictable, all night. I try to focus on falling asleep. Then, with the effort of doing so, I wake.

3

In the middle of the night – the real night – Anne flung open the door. She was the kind of mother who refused to knock. A fan of borders but not boundaries.

They've dug up *all* the courgettes, she said.

The moles?

Much worse. Forget the moles.

Neither of us moved.

Come on – she flipped the lights – we're being besieged. Get a shovel. Anya you can hold a torch.

Michael refused to be routed. I heard him insist Anne respect his sleep – she was more than intimidating enough to handle marauding boar.

Outside, we took in the destruction. Mounds of earth uprooted, shredded plants, craters, gougings and tracks disfiguring the lawn.

Monsters, she spat.

It's not their fault, Luke said.

Whose is it then?

They were hunted to extinction then reintroduced. Deliberately. By *us*.

I never introduced pigs to my garden.

They were here first, then we killed them off and got nostalgic for it.

Luke. I'm an animal person so spare me the sermon, please. But this – she gestured around. This is ridiculous. They go after dogs. They laid waste to Pem's farm. Last time I heard one run along the decking I leant out the window and shot it. It was like a bomb going off. All the mud and dust. Took four of us to put it in Pem's truck. Very good meat, so it was probably worth the carnage, in the end.

Luke stopped digging, closed his eyes and exhaled.

Your mum's – she seems manic, I whispered. Do you think we – you – should make her lie down?

He mumbled something about going to get a glass of water but never came back. I finished our end of the trench alone.

After several hours digging, erecting fortifications using upturned chairs, I realised I was enjoying myself. I felt useful working alongside Anne, and it reminded me of my childhood, when anything could be reimagined into something new. Shoes became firewood, sheets became windows, my brother's skateboard became a water cart.

But the objects I gravitated toward aesthetically now, I realised as I positioned two dining chairs like coping stones, all had an underlying stability. The sculptural things I collected maybe did have emotional resonance then, in that I couldn't imagine them transmuting into anything else.

Finally Anne surveyed the barricades. Seagulls called overhead and I followed her gaze to where the perimeter disappeared into the dawn mist and then the creek.

That should do it, she said. For now at least.

I crept back into bed beside Luke and admired the crescents of black dirt under my nails. I kissed the warm skin at the back of his neck. Then I remembered the poisoned trees.

Luke drank several cups of coffee at breakfast, rubbing his face and the back of his head. I was used to surviving on no sleep, but he needed at least eight hours to make any conversation. I loaded the dishwasher and pretended not to notice as Anne restacked everything.

I thought, she said slowly as she closed the machine, we'd take a walk to the church.

We put boots on and followed her and Michael along the road past the Spar. Another new house had been built, its glass front loomed behind a row of white saplings, spectral as a mushroom. Like the others in their vicinity, it appeared to be empty.

Can't understand why anyone would want to live under *glass*, she hissed. The few times I've actually seen someone in there, well, you can see *everything*. At night especially, I can see all its insides, like a jellyfish. There are more and more, they attract each other, these planning notices – she pointed to one pinned to the gate – like a swarm.

I imagined Anne standing outside the house in the dark. I agreed it was out of place.

We passed the disused garage, overgrown by weeds. Here Luke, an only child, had founded his own clubhouse after reading *Lord of the Flies*. Still his favourite book. And of course, as Anne was fond of pointing out, another Cornish author. There was still genitalia-themed graffiti in the basement and a shrivelled buoy hung from a steel joist to make a swing. On the upper level, where cars were repaired, there were stepped walls on three sides like a theatre, which must have lent gravity to meetings. Luke confessed they used to defecate in the long grass behind rather than return to the cottage where his mother remained in charge.

I followed Luke's gaze toward it, it was clear he wanted to go inside.

Go on ahead, we'll catch you up, he told his parents.

I didn't like going in there, but I liked it that Luke wanted to go in. It suggested a continued wish to escape his mother's influence.

There was no glass in the window frames and it smelt of decay. Sometimes I seek that basement smell out precisely because I don't like it. It's still familiar. Cold concrete and earth.

We rejoined them in the graveyard. Anne took me through her thoughts on floral arrangements. I looked in Luke's direction, wondering if he would mention the idea we'd come to the night his friends had interrogated us, of having a non-religious ceremony with Christopher as our celebrant. I knew the only gay men Anne had ever knowingly met were two Canadians. Rather than say the word she now referred to all gay people as being *like the Canadian men*.

Michael pointed out the usual headstone belonging to their family. I spotted a magpie dart away beyond it and looked for a second. On a similar walk, long ago, Anne had stopped abruptly before one and saluted him in the middle of the road. Not understanding, I'd reacted with nervous laughter. That Christmas she gave me *A Pocket Guide to the Superstitions of the British Isles*. They're othering you, Christopher had said. Give her one for the Balkans next year.

The church was dismal. Michael disappeared and a few electric lights came on. I sensed Luke waiting for me to say something before he would. Then into the resonant silence, Michael's voice:

Not much trade except funerals these days.

Luke appeared to be avoiding eye contact with me now and I panicked.

I love it here, I lied.

Wonderful, Anne said, that settles it then.

Going back, we took a longer route off-road. Gradually the path narrowed so that we walked in single file. I felt myself detaching, following Luke's calves, letting them get further ahead until finally they were gone.

When I arrived back at the cottage, they were seated in a ring on the lawn which still bore the scars of the previous night. Luke was describing our holiday and the town of Sanary where many artists and writers had exiled themselves as Hitler rose to power.

Aldous Huxley, Thomas Mann, Bertolt Brecht, Stefan Zweig, he trailed off.

Sybille Bedford, I continued.

Don't know her, Anne said.

I said I would give her one of Bedford's books. Maybe *Quicksands*. I realised I did not want to share with them her impressions of Yugoslavia from *Pleasures and Landscapes*. Though much of it was admiring – the mountains, Venetian architecture, translucent water – I'd experienced the familiar contraction around my chest as I read her descriptions of the terrifying roads and wild children on the ferry crossing:

> What one wonders about is the future. Will it be a graceless, stark new world?

And finally of her time in Sarajevo,

> nothing ever, perhaps, quite safe, quite clean, quite straight . . .

Bedford, I told them, lived out the Holocaust in Sanary, later California. I heard my words echo what I'd read about her, sounding fluent. I understood her ambivalence at having spent so much time reading in comfortable places.

Anne and Michael wanted to see my photos. Luke had told them I'd taken several hundred. This was true. He rarely recorded anything on his phone except runs and photographs of plants.

They admired my pictures of the villa, the pink oleander, the view of the bay, Luke's kitesurfing technique, the harmonious blue of the water, tasteful market stalls, a fish we ate at the Hôtel de la Tour that had baked inside a white salt crust and was then exhumed for us at the table.

Doesn't look as flashy as you'd expect, Anne said, approving.

If their family went to restaurants, she would instruct everyone to order the same thing, since that way it was more like being at home. It was one of the things I felt I offered Luke, permission to indulge his yuppie side – to go out and order whatever he wanted.

Luke said there were no gin palaces in the harbour, a section of which was occupied by traditional fishing boats. He said there were few tourists, other than French from the north, and it was, compared to the surrounding destinations British holidaymakers had heard of, unspoiled.

Then he told the Bedford anecdote I'd relayed to him, concerning the Huxleys' arrival. Looking forward to the anonymity of a foreign place, Maria and Aldous had pulled up at their new Belle Époque home to find VILLA HULEY painted in bold lettering by the well-meaning decorator on the front gate. I knew why this resonated for Luke, who was horrified by the idea of public spectacle. It was something we'd discussed with regard to the wedding, he wanted the minimum possible number of guests. I was fine with that. Relieved, actually. It was easier to describe a wedding as intimate than find the words to explain why no one from my family would be there.

Anne held out my phone. I felt her gaze linger on the ring as I took it back and felt hot as if I'd stolen it.

She offered around segments from a clementine which I declined, though not before Luke could remind her of my hang-up.

The excuse I usually gave was not a lie, exactly. I *had* been eating plums gathered from the base of my grandmother's tree as a child. I *had* accidentally picked up part of a bird, ripped open, the greasy remains now heaving with life. I *had* been horrified by the sticky mess, its texture in my hand, the apprehension of anarchy.

The sight of some fruit can affect me like an animal whose fur is rubbed against its growth. Perhaps reasonably, given the nature of his work, Luke found this fact exasperating. Even *seedless* grapes? he would ask in perplexity as I declined to follow him down certain supermarket aisles.

As a child I dreamt about exotic fruit I knew only from cartoons. Sometimes we got parcels with exciting things and we'd make them last for weeks. Other times we got biscuits from WW2 and we'd feel resentful of the kids on other streets. I wanted Coca-Cola so badly that I hate it now. The same thing happened when I finally tried tinned pineapple and choked on the wet, syrupy chunks. In my mind, the longed-for fruit had the texture of human flesh.

The smell is fine. Maybe I've been desensitised by synthetic fruit-scented things. I can even enjoy fruit flavours, as long as there is no remnant of the original texture there. But the thought of biting directly into a tomato or unmediated slice of orange makes me gag. The various sensations that combine in the average piece of fruit! Seed, liquid, flesh, skin . . .

In the afternoon Luke caught up on sleep, forgetting to take the meat for dinner out of the freezer as he'd promised Anne to do. I remembered too late, and had to massage it beside the fire while he slept and his mother was busy somewhere in the garden. I was still attempting to defrost it when she came in and saw me there, crouching. When he came down I was silently angry that he'd left me open to his mother's suspicion of being a barbarian, and as we finally sat down to eat, much later than planned, we seemed to be engaged in another psychic stand-off. I did not know why he was angry at *me*. I had saved the day. I remember hoping those vicissitudes in personality were chemical. A lighthouse whose beam disappeared only to come back.

Normal people argue, I said once, and then we had a very quiet argument in the garden centre, beside an LED Buddha fountain and a sign that read TRANQUIL OASIS. I felt such relief despite the humidity, the claustrophobia, the smell of rabbit hutch. His moods would shift abruptly, and at times I would find myself having crossed an obscure boundary into a strange place, a territory which only minutes ago had not been there.

The change could be even subtler. A shadow over the sun, a cold spot in water. Swimming as a child, I remembered turning onto my back, putting trust in the sky, imagining I swam in that element instead.

Luke could be two people as distinct as these elements, just as he had two names in my phone. Real name to indicate company mobile and pet name for personal. Depending on which he called from, our conversation would be altered.

At first I hadn't noticed the second person. I began to, soon after I moved in. Around the time things started to go wrong in the flat. The bath plug lost its suction. I couldn't fill the bath with water unless I kept it running, and even then, it would only reach my hips. A shelf came off the wall. A chair back marked another with a groove. The tap – which Luke had never had a problem with before – now leaked, heavy and staccato through the night. A gas ring refused to ignite. Clicking over and over without producing a flame. These went on a list of things to be fixed, and everything else on a list to break.

After dinner we watched the news and the mood lifted. They liked working out the BBC's more obscure visual puns. A story about pressure on primary school places was accompanied by seemingly unrelated footage of rowers, then canoes, and then the Queen's barge moving down the Thames. The connection between these images and the news story remained a mystery until the reporter ended with the words: The race is on.

Ho ho, Michael said.

Luke held my foot under a cushion then took one of my hands. They were covered in soot after poking the fire to thaw the meat, my fingers stained purple from chopping red cabbage. I'd removed the ring to prepare the food – an absence he mutely noted as he examined them. I tipped my head back to indicate where I'd put it. Then the news came to Brexit and I felt the room contract.

His parents knew which way I'd voted, but we hadn't directly talked about it since. They didn't know I'd exchanged insults with strangers on the internet late into the night. The 'real' people, with whom I'd argue until confronted with my own unreality, my own irrelevance. It was not the specifics of opposing arguments that upset me, but that the things I held on to, which kept me from being sucked back into the past, were coming loose.

Because my aunt was not my mother, when I'd had disputes with her children, they felt she was biased toward me and I felt she was biased toward them. Her son Nikolaj was a compulsive liar who had a problem with authority, except where it gave him power. He hated me not only for being clever, despite the language disadvantage, but because I'd experienced things he had not. I didn't understand then that he felt threatened. Not just by having to share his family with strangers, though that didn't help, but because in comparison to mine his life story was a domestic drama. He'd take great pleasure in warping events with unnecessary lies so that our referee, his mother, would eventually wave us away: *carry on for all I care, just stay out of my kitchen*. My sister Daria left for university a few months after we arrived, and then I had no one to confirm what I'd seen or heard versus what he then said had happened.

Why did I want things to stay the same? Christopher, who'd spoiled his ballot, asked me. He has an anarchist streak but somehow ended up a lawyer. A human rights barrister, more accurately. Law was what his parents had wanted him to do, and perhaps because of his ability to stand outside or above any such man-made edifice, he was very good.

I didn't have an answer for him. It was an emotion I couldn't put into adequate words. I remember right before the referendum, another wedding, this time Luke's non-Cornish cousin's, on Michael's side, I'd been seated next to a man I didn't know. One of the groom's parents' friends. He didn't know *anyone*, he claimed, which initially seemed the reason for our pairing. Then he said he was a poet, as well as a writer of thrillers for which he used a pseudonym. He pointed knowingly at my surname on the place card. He asked me about my parents, their ethnicity, and I said I was the child of a mixed marriage. In his capacity as a poet, he had travelled to the Balkans, and so for most of the reception, wanted to talk about the war.

I detected that tone I so often encountered then. As though such chaos could never occur within his island, whereas in the Balkans it was inevitable. Luke had later sympathised when I complained about my table, saying he understood how maddening it was – in the context of anthropogenic climate change. He called it the blind spot of any culture – the inability to conceive of its own destruction.

Occasionally I'd made attempts to engage the neighbour on my other side, an elderly relative of the bride's. She'd blinked at me kindly and said it must be sad when your country no longer exists, then returned to pulverising her asparagus. The need for discretion removed, the poet began to list his top ten most harrowing sights. His lips were wet. He topped up my glass and said that history must not repeat itself. That though the EU was imperfect, like Yugoslavia, like any marriage in fact, British people valued what it represented. Membership, he mused as a server took our plates away, was probably my homeland's only hope. We had better get a move on with integration.

A year on, if someone raised the subject in my presence I felt myself shut down. I couldn't bear to meet people's outrage or smirking faces, even their shock and grief. If it was mentioned at a party, whether or not I'd had anything to drink, I would simply walk away. Now I felt myself sliding into apathy.

On Sunday morning Luke kissed my shoulder tenderly then got up, pulled on his shorts and went running. I stayed in bed, the windows open, listening to the gentle call of a wood pigeon. The room flooded with light and a breeze came in off the creek. I'd had my first unbroken sleep in weeks and the combination of breeze, sunlight and memory foam gave me the sensation of gliding. Suddenly I heard the strains of what I took to be a recording of a piece of classical music. It began with tuning, but then, from its occasional repetitions, stops and starts, I understood that it was live.

I guessed a group of students were rehearsing, but I'd never seen any young people when I'd stayed before. My only explanation was that one of the elderly neighbours, or maybe the very rich one who poisoned trees, had convened a small orchestra, not for any reason other than enjoyment. Something about this idea seemed incredible. Though I did very little in the way of making money – did very little generally – I found it hard to think in any terms other than productivity.

As the communal effort of several brass instruments sailed into the room, a feeling of contentment and security verging on euphoria coursed through me. I stretched my limbs toward the four corners of the bed and felt a desire that I'd forgotten. I wanted to have sex with Luke.

I remained in that position for several more minutes with my eyes closed, listening to what I guessed was a cello, letting it merge with the wind, the heat of my skin. I sensed this was a moment I could have only once. When it stopped I'd never know what the piece I'd been listening to was. I thought of its transience, of using it up, like precious water running.

The solo ended and the silence which followed sounded entirely different from the silence that had preceded it, as if it was now part of something else.

I didn't know much about classical music and wondered if I should admit to this in order to ask Michael if he'd heard and could identify the piece for me. To risk being told it was something obvious.

He had extensive knowledge of all genres. The search function on iTunes had proved endlessly absorbing. He spent hours on these voyages of discovery, back and forth in time, through world music, thrash and electronica. He'd made Luke four CDs composed of songs with American cities in the title for no reason other than the search function made it possible. They had been good for long car journeys before we discovered true crime. Some were classics, others by obscure heavy metal groups we knew to skip past.

He had unofficially taken charge of wedding music and given us a list that included a Cornish folksong arranged by Holst. The lyrics describe a woman released from bedlam by her lover who has returned from being at sea. I wondered if Michael had recalled the part about it being the man's parents who'd tried to keep her institutionalised.

I rolled over on the bed to the window, pulled myself onto my knees and crouched forward with my elbows on the sill to wait for him, watching the Optimists sail past the mouth of the creek, remembering the time Luke had insisted on taking me sailing. They could not believe I'd never been before, until I got into the boat.

Now I heard Michael's voice. He and Anne were standing below the window. I shot back, covering my chest. Thinking they must've heard me, I prepared to call out a greeting, but a prickling heat rose across my skin and I closed my mouth again.

I've looked. Nothing comes up. Nothing I can make sense of anyway. I really think it's odd Luke's never met them. I know he says they're just not close but I'm beginning to think it's more really.

Snip.

More than she's let on you mean?

For a few moments I was paralysed.

. . . contribution . . .

. . . never . . .

. . . marquee . . .

Snip.

If that's what he wants.

Snip snip.

. . . clever seating plan . . .

Sometimes I could hear whole sentences very clearly, other times only random words as they moved with secateurs along the trellis against the wall. They must've assumed we'd gone together – but would see when Luke came back he was alone. Given the open window, it would look like I'd been listening, and I knew I wouldn't be able to pretend I hadn't heard.

I put my hands over my ears, then pulled the covers over my head but could still detect certain words. I longed to close the window but forced myself to be still.

Savages,

If they come,

Children,

Communists,

Christmas,

I told you,

Stuck with it darling.

I pressed harder into the pillow. Trapped there, with my eyes closed, I could almost see the words as illuminated streaks firing through the window.

When Luke got back I said I had a headache and needed to stay in bed. I gave the kind of vague explanation

– fine, tired – he always gave that drove me mad when I knew something else was wrong. I didn't come down for lunch and saw Anne and Michael only to murmur bye and thanks as we put our bags into the car.

On the motorway I was silent, listening to the murder Luke put on – a woman who'd stabbed her fiancé in the heart with a steak knife – until we stopped for fuel. Luke bought food from Marks and Spencer which we ate across the dashboard. When we'd finished, I slotted the oily containers one inside the other, and asked if he still wanted to meet my family.

SPLIT

4

You can't fly direct to Sarajevo from London. We decided to take a connecting flight on the way back (using Luke's preferred calculator to determine the carbon footprint and how much reforestation would offset it) but on the outward journey chose to fly to Split instead, where we'd rent a car and drive along the Croatian coast for a few days (what Luke called a holiday and Christopher called assimilation), then head inland to stay with my parents.

The night before we were due to fly I crawled out of bed, staggered to the bathroom and lay with my cheek against the cold tiles before reaching my arms around the toilet to be sick.

When I stood, the walls disintegrated and I was sick again, depositing, into the basin this time, the little food I'd eaten. I stared for a minute, then tried to wash everything down, succeeding only in blocking the pipe. The sink began to fill. Sensing the end was far away, I hobbled out for a bucket and rug, teeth chattering, then sat back on the bathroom floor to ride things out.

When Luke's alarm sounded at five, I felt too weak to call between rooms, so stayed there on the floor, waiting for him to find me.

What are you doing down there, he said, reaching over me for his towel.

Sick, I whispered, jaw rigid.

My mouth barely moved but still the effort produced another spasm. I raised my hand in warning. I thought of that gesture in religious paintings. *Noli me tangere*.

Luke said we didn't have to go. Or didn't have to go that day. I hadn't slept, the flights were cheap, we could always catch another. I said I suspected I'd feel the same way until I got there. That though I still felt nauseous I'd passed the bile stage and didn't have anything left inside me to eject.

I'm not prone to action, but once I do commit I find I can't change course. I'd consulted Christopher about the trip. It might be good to make things normal, he'd advised.

We had to leave the blocked drain for when we got back.

Luke got an Uber to take us to the station and from there we boarded the airport express, where my ashen face did not stand out from the other passengers headed for early flights with other budget airlines.

He got me a seat facing forward and began to make a circular stroking motion on the back of my hand. I shook him off.

He nodded and turned back to his phone while I sat, straight-backed, taking small sips of water.

At the airport he checked in our shared suitcase and I responded to Christopher's chirpy *bon voyage*, thumbs shaking. *Already a nightmare*, I typed.

After security we navigated the speciously winding path through A WORLD OF BRANDS. Salespeople in black menaced us with perfume and Luke steered them away protectively. Ahead of us a figure in an unidentifiable animal suit lurched toward small children and their parents, listlessly waving a Union Jack.

Waiting on the transit bus, I studied faces. Some were young couples going on holiday, familiar in that they looked like us, but then I noticed others, perhaps returning. Strangers with faces I somehow knew.

Our seats were in the middle of the plane and as we shunted past each row, the sight of so much irradiated human flesh made me convulse again. Luke gave me his aisle seat so I could make a swift exit, just in case, and he took the middle one. When the seatbelt signs turned on we realised no passenger had claimed the window so Luke shifted over, leaving the seat between us empty.

I placed my water, phone, book and A4 thesis notebook on the empty seat (with the fantastic notion I might feel better and want to work) until a stewardess told me to hold or stow all of these away. I knew I couldn't tolerate holding water as it sloshed about, and I couldn't face bending over or standing up again, so placed the items inside the leather pocket in front. I remember telling myself not to leave them behind, which was something I usually told Luke, who was always losing things. The stewardess then asked if we were aware that ours was the emergency exit row, and whether Luke was prepared to open the door in the event of emergency.

Her make-up sat thick and matte over her face, while the back of her neck and behind her ears, where her hair was pulled tightly into a doughnut, was pale and shimmered with blue veins. It seemed less like make-up than an actual mask. I imagined that behind it she despised her job, which involved making so many life-saving announcements and yet never being listened to. She carried on down the aisle. Whether they knew it or not, the surrounding passengers, like myself, now had no choice but to place their faith in Luke. The idea distracted me a little from the nausea. I glanced at the rows of waxen faces, strange companions in this aluminium tube, with a new feeling of shared destiny, or powerlessness.

Then it occurred to me that any one of these captive strangers might yank the emergency door in a suicidal act. I closed my eyes and felt the plane start to roll away from its moorings.

When I opened them again Luke had started reading my copy of the Rebecca West. He'd asked if he could borrow it, if I thought it would be good to read, and I'd said yes without admitting I'd never read it. I'd filled whole shelves with books about the Balkans but couldn't bring myself to open any. I'd told myself that on my thirtieth birthday I would finally begin to read them as a symbolic transition into adulthood, having respectfully observed something like a governmental thirty-year-rule. I was thirty-one by then.

I felt the ground begin moving, vibrating through my feet. I had to lift them off the floor but that also made me dizzy. An acrid taste coated my throat as we rose up and into the air.

I fell asleep at some point and woke to find the cabin peacefully aglow. The stewards were making their way along the aisle with the trolley. I looked at Luke, still absorbed in Rebecca West. The sun shot through the window, bleaching the fibrous edges of the page. His face, where he hadn't shaved, was haloed with white fuzz. Beyond him the sky. Our plane was its sole occupant, and I felt my stomach relax for the first time since the pain had woken me in the night. By keeping my gaze steadily on the blue, its refuge at once a private and unbounded space, it was possible to forget the confined one in which I sat, the proximity to treacherous neighbours.

Then I heard a small thud. My feet felt the reverberation too. I started and looked down. A dark, compact object had appeared beneath the seat in front. Unwilling to risk renewed nausea by bending forward, I watched as a woman's arm emerged, followed by her upper body which bulged around the armrest before becoming trapped. A hand groped on the floor beside her for what I now saw, with horror, was a navy plum.

The woman was too wide to extend far enough out of her seat to retrieve it, and the seatbelt signs remained lit. The plum rolled toward my foot. I felt the muscles in my stomach tighten. As the plane turned slightly, the plum rolled hopefully toward the stranger's hand, then back again toward my foot.

Luke, I murmured, unable to raise my voice above the engine and the rushing in my ears.

Luke – please –

He appeared not to hear, or maybe he just ignored me. I couldn't look away from the plum, throbbing on the floor like a grenade.

Sometimes language helps in these situations. Not articulating what I'm feeling, but putting the scene into words as if I was transcribing it, separating me from the experience. I put the different elements into separate lexical sets. The plum rolled against my foot. An explosion. Seeds, skin, liquid, flesh. I thought about the etymology of *grenade*. In French it means pomegranate, after which the explosive is named.

A slow tear slid around my cheek and without warning, I saw the toe of my own shoe kick the plum away from me.

A gasp.

A pause.

Then the plum owner's eye emerged in the slit between the seats in front, swivelling from Luke, hidden behind the enormous book, across the empty seat, to me. It narrowed as she took in my appearance, calibrating her response.

Well thanks, she said at last. Thanks *very* much. Can't fucking eat it now, can I?

Luke shot a hostile glance in my direction but otherwise pretended not to know who I was.

A muscle in my eye quivered. Since this was out of character my brain could not admit guilt. I took a deep breath and shut both eyes until the woman stopped speaking in my direction and began complaining about our disintegrating social contract to her neighbour.

Everyone just looks out for themselves now, don't they?

I went back to my view, but another plane was visible now. It hovered like our plane's shadow on a bright blue floor. This changed the way I'd interpreted the scene before. Now the emptiness felt exposing. I was desperate to get off the plane.

The second, miniaturised one changed the nature of our aircraft as well as the sky we travelled through. No longer containers for human transportation, but sentient beings almost. The pair seemed conscious of each other, and not merely in that they registered on their respective radar screens.

I wondered about the people on board the other. What, if anything, any of them made of us. But then the second plane rolled away or ours veered slightly to the right and in an instant the sky was empty. Once its wake had dissipated, it was as if neither the slow, synchronised dance, nor it, had ever existed.

At Split Airport, Luke walked up the jet bridge to the terminal ahead of me, carrying my small bag as well as his backpack. I stared at his back with a feeling of tenderness. How well I knew it. Watching his long, purposeful strides I felt unusually light, carrying nothing in my hands or on my shoulders, and optimism swelled inside me.

I watched him move through the double set of motion sensor doors that sealed the terminal from its points of entry, and followed him through, enjoying the way the two panels pulled apart in quick succession with a curving mechanism. The moment I passed through the final doors and heard them swish behind me, I knew I'd forgotten the items I'd stored in the seat in front of mine.

I stopped abruptly. My whole body seized up. The person behind rammed into me but I stayed rigid. I called to Luke, who continued marching ahead, before I took a few reluctant steps toward where he was already rounding the first bend of a ramp to immigration and connecting flights. I stopped again and turned back toward the doors, above which were written, in several languages: DO NOT STOP, DO NOT RETURN.

I waited for a few minutes like a cat, watching people pass through, judging the brief pause between the first closing and the second opening, looking for an opportunity to push back through, the precise manoeuvre such doors are designed to prevent.

Then I felt my arm restrained above the elbow and Luke appeared at my side.

My book's in the seat, I said, stumbling. And my phone. Which has everything. But the book has *everything*, everything. Everything for my, every – all in there. Actually – too – but mainly—

Luke patted his backpack, I've got the book.

I was confused for a moment.

No. The other one. My thesis.

Oh that.

He sounded irritated. I stared past him in disbelief. How could I have done this?

Well the phone's backed up right?

I don't know.

How can you not know?

I don't even know what that means.

His thumb dug painfully into bone, pulling me away from the people trying to get by. There was no way he was letting me try to get back to the plane. I'd get stuck, or shot, he promised, looking warily around. We'd be better off presenting ourselves to one of the kiosks beyond passport control, getting them to call someone on the plane. I kept staring at him. He stared back. I thought about pulling my arm from him and making a run for it but my legs were rooted.

Come on, he said decisively, the irritation checked. It's not lost, OK? We'll get it back.

I pressed the heels of my hands into my eyes and stood like that for another minute, then let myself be guided down the ramp.

I could count three times I'd lost anything of any value through my own carelessness. My first mobile phone – taken from a leisure centre in Glasgow. A twenty-pound note – escaped from the back pocket of fitted jeans while protesting war against Iraq. A cache of used film – when my bag disappeared at an airport. Each a devastation.

I didn't understand how some people seemed to lose things so often and hardly react. Because I was the kind of person who did not lose things, on the rare occasions I did, I too felt lost.

You're exhausted, he said. You were up all night. It's not your fault.

As we stood in line to show our passports, I raked a nail along my jaw as he told me about the doorway effect. Moving to the kitchen from another room, we forget what we were looking for as we pass through the door or open a cupboard. Our brain is wiped clean in that new place. What had just happened to me was the reverse, he said. It was passing through the door that had unfrozen the memory of what I'd left on the other side of it.

Everybody loses things on planes, he concluded as our passports were handed back.

Well I don't, I said, forcing myself to stop scratching at my skin. I never have.

And you haven't now, I mean. We're going to get it back.

The man behind the glass at the counter for airport enquiries and lost property was dressed as if he took his role extremely seriously. His hair was slicked back and a tie clip glinted on his narrow chest. I hadn't been prepared for this conversation, and when I opened my mouth no words came out. Without the lost things, or in this place without them, my brain seemed to be malfunctioning. I pulled my hands slowly down my face, digging into my cheeks. Tears came but I didn't cry.

Officially, the language I was trying to speak no longer exists. Now there are four names for four dialects, though anyone who speaks one can understand the rest. There's a meme of a cigarette packet that bears the words SMOKING KILLS. Twice in the Latin script and once in Cyrillic. The spelling is exactly the same for each.

Breathe, Luke said.

Sorry, I said, observing the man as he made some new calculation as to who the young woman before him was, speaking rusty Serbo-Croat.

I handed over the stub of my boarding pass and watched his expression change and then change again as he called the aircraft. I understood that he spoke with a woman who had gone to check my seat. I held on to the counter to stop from scratching at my chin.

She says it's not there.

I closed my eyes.

Anya, you were sitting in my seat, did you give them my seat number?

Yes, I said irritably, realising that I hadn't.

Luke gave me a suspicious look as I added this information.

Not there either, she says.

I placed my hand over my stomach.

Tell her . . .

No phone has been found.

I clenched my fists.

Tell them the book is black and smooth, very smooth. It would feel the same as the magazines and . . . cards. She has to open it, the seat pocket, and look.

He spoke further with the voice on the other end, looking at me, then hung up the receiver and shook his head.

Please fill out this form.

I wrenched the chained ballpoint and tried to contain the urge to scream. In that moment, it seemed preferable to be trapped in limbo between the two security doors than here, free, without the lost items. I felt betrayed by Luke's caution, wishing I'd followed my own rash instinct to run back.

What's that supposed to be? Luke said, peering at my cross-hatchings.

In addition to filling out my details I'd used some of the blank space to draw a picture of my A4 notebook. The drawing described the situation in three composite ways. Appearance (black, rectangular), silhouette (black, rectangular), absence, and my feelings about that.

What was in your book? the man asked with new curiosity.

I gave him the form, blotting my eyes with a sleeve.

Everything, I said dramatically. My life.

He slotted the form into a folder – whose flap I could make out said LOST.

I pictured the little beige counter this man presided over, with his shiny hair and tie, his hitherto indifferent manner, as having been set up at the end of the car hire and currency exchange kiosks not as a place to retrieve physical belongings (which evidently was not its chief success) but as a means of rehabilitation to the state of losing things.

I thought about how recovery is the opposite of loss, and how the word, in my adopted language at least, contained the two senses – to have returned and to heal – often, though not always, one and the same thing.

It also occurred to me that it might have been the first time I'd seen Luke at a disadvantage. He did not have a mother tongue with which to exclude me now, except in the native language of his body. Here the scales had tipped a little. It was a new sensation, to know he was reliant on me.

It now seemed impossible that at one time I could barely speak his language. Long before I met him. Still a child. Or more childlike. I had made learning it the focus of my life. I said so at my undergraduate interview, going full tilt.

Why English?

The professors were too awkward to ask much more than that, but I know my English teacher, who'd encouraged me to apply there, must have told them something in her reference.

Luke went to get the car and I waited for our shared black case. The same bags came past over and over. Round the carousel in a figure of eight. I felt the tiny surge of semantic power extinguished. My thoughts kept looping back to the lost items, regretting having come, then a self-loathing that energised me briefly, before remembering the purpose of the trip. In essence, to ensure life didn't turn out like this: a lone woman waiting, unable to pay proper attention, her personal property slipping from reach.

At last our bag dropped down the chute. I made a pact with myself not to bore Luke about the missing things, aiming for temporary amnesia until we made it back to London. Only once I'd decided this did the practical consequences register. I didn't know my parents' or sister's number by heart, or even their address. They'd moved again, apparently, this time back to our old neighbourhood.

I joined Luke, still negotiating car rental, and asked to borrow his phone.

Why?

My parents' address.

What for? We're not going there now, first, are we?

In the car, he keyed our Dubrovnik address into the map. I said I was feeling more normal again, nausea-wise, and so we decided on the scenic route that twisted round every bay along the coast. Once our route was decided, he passed the phone to me but I couldn't log into my email. Luke, ever security conscious, had insisted I activate Google's two-step verification, which required inputting a passcode that was sent to your phone.

How else can we do this? he said over the satnav's voice. Is the address written some—

He was about to suggest my notebook but stopped himself in time.

We did a second tour of the roundabout by mistake. The obvious person to call would have been my aunt, but again – no contact for her without my phone. I thought about trying to reach one of her children on social media. Luke had quit all his and had pressured me into quitting too, but I knew they could be reactivated.

The idea filled me with dread. As far as I was aware the two daughters, Diana and Tamara, lived in Dubai these days. Nikolaj, or Calum as he went by now, either did not have Facebook or never sent a friend request. I shrunk from the thought of having to explain myself and why I did not know my parents' address. Why I was coming back. I didn't want them to know anything about me. I didn't want that part of my life to know Luke existed. I thought of his reluctance to hand his phone over again and felt the familiar tug of possessiveness.

What about friends?

I blinked and looked down at the phone.

I could sense the realisation dawning on him that the minutes we'd spent digesting this administrative problem, broached on a Croatian dual carriageway while our overlord barked NEXT EXIT, had occasioned greater insight into my past than we'd managed in the most intimate conversations of our relationship over the previous five years.

For a long time my sister and I couldn't go back. First because war was still going on, then so as not to jeopardise our status. My parents became voices inside a beige receiver. One time after I spoke to them, I heard my aunt suggesting to my mother that they join us in Scotland. This was something I'd asked them to do, twice, in a letter and in a phone call; both times it had been dismissed, but hearing it in her mouth made me realise it was a valid question.

I don't know what my mother said, but from my aunt's side it was clearly unsatisfactory. Think of your children. Of Drago. Those people are not your family.

You don't owe them this loyalty. My mother must have said something harsh in response, because the pleading tone changed and the conversation ended.

By the time I arrived at university, where everyone was away from home, I could imagine it no other way. We continued phone calls – a monthly check-in as unremarkable as menstruation – meaning only that nothing there had changed. I asked them the same litany of questions and if they started to veer off script, I would find a way to cut the conversation short, citing an essay deadline or lecture, some shiny facet of my new intellectual life – the bourgeois exile they'd arranged for me for all their talk of *brotherhood and unity*. Sometimes I was callous. I didn't want to hear anything that would make me feel bad. Sometimes I said things to estrange them purposefully, like wishing them a Merry Christmas.

Mira! I said finally, startling him after a long silence. Mira.

Mira. OK. Who's that?

He turned to me expectantly, but I was busy searching her name.

Mira was my brother's girlfriend, his fiancée in the end, and the last time I'd seen her was at his funeral nearly a decade ago. 2008. I was curious to see how things had turned out for her since that year of turmoil. She'd been his age, twenty-six. I was approaching my first graduation and remembered how she gripped my hand as she told me her plans. She was going to move to Belgrade. She had completed a Masters, spoke three languages, but was working as a nanny. I avoided talking about my brother. Her grief felt private, removed from our shared history.

Her family lived in the same apartment block as mine when the only people we could stay in touch with were our immediate neighbours. Everyone else might as well have been on another planet, though there were only streets between us. We played games in the basement and the hallway when we couldn't go outside. That group of kids we were part of – all ages – had become family.

Like my brother, I'd had a crush on Mira. I gave her my last piece of Čunga Lunga, only to discover it had made its way to him. When I cried he gave the gum back to her, and she to me, telling me I should savour it, divide it into pieces and chew each one until all the taste was gone. I was ashamed of crying and I wanted to show her I could be defiant, reckless like my brother who liked to tease the snipers. I remember her eyes flashing as the bright blue square disappeared inside my mouth.

She started calling me her sister after that. A ten-year gap meant my own regarded me as a burden on her freedom. Mira, who had no siblings, derived great pleasure from me – braiding my hair and helping to furnish my dolls with clothes – and I preferred to be infantilised by her rather than act grown-up for my actual sister. We played marbles when Drago was reading Alan Ford.

They began calling themselves boyfriend and girlfriend although they were only eleven. It seemed intoxicatingly mature to me, and at first it had strained basement relations with her parents, hers being less permissive, but Drago was so devoted to her throughout that period, and after as far as I know, that soon they too were in love with my brother.

It was very chaste, but I heard my mother caution him that she'd had Daria by accident too young and Drago had looked horrified by the insinuation.

My parents weren't married when they had my sister. But when Daria was four, Mum proposed to Dad – not long before Tito died. The day after their wedding was spent reading the newspapers and following his state funeral in a stupor. Drago used to remind us both with a haughty look that while Daria and I were mistakes, implicitly the product of erratic lovemaking, he – the halfway mark between both errors – was the only child they had planned. Somehow this was less horrifying.

The marriage had been open, though not without jealousy. Even before the siege I'd got used to waiting with increasing foreboding for one or other of them to come home, or being bundled out of bed still in my pyjamas. My mother would take us to one of the neighbours and disappear into the night, or, worse, bring me with her so I could press the buzzer and ask for my father back. One of my earliest memories is coming into the living room in the night only to find a strange man on the sofa with his trousers down, my mother kneeling. Me and my siblings were the go-betweens, delivering entreaties or threats, depending on which of us was enlisted.

I knew from rare conversations with my sister that Mira's Belgrade plan had worked out, but still I was surprised to find that she was the first search result returned for Mira Panić. The one I clicked on first, halfway down, produced a Bad Gateway, but her company profile listed a work email and a direct line.

Calling felt intrusive. Unnerving for me, too, with Luke sitting there, even if he couldn't understand. Instead I wrote a short email from Luke's account before I had time to overthink it, then fell instantly into a deep, remedial sleep, rocked by the winding road.

When I woke Luke was tapping my shoulder. The car was stationary.

Passports.

He looked agitated, indicating a checkpoint several cars ahead.

We're about to drive through Bosnia for six miles, he continued as I came round, then out again. I think.

He cocked his head at the map. We were indeed about to pass through the tiny stretch of BiH coast. Those twelve miles now separate the northern part of Croatia from Dubrovnik.

On leaving Croatia, the Bosnian officers gave us a cursory glance through the window and waved us through. Luke shifted in his seat, peering at the terracotta roofs and identical sloping foothills as if trying to detect some slight variation. Minutes later, we arrived at the checkpoint to re-enter Croatia again. The Croatian guard solemnly inspected our passports and the details of the hire car for several minutes before allowing us to continue. As we pulled away Luke checked his rear mirror and said:

That was mad.

Just symbolic.

He turned to me, eyebrows raised.

And mad. Of course.

Then his phone vibrated.

I'd forgotten the email I'd sent before falling asleep. Mira was *delighted* to hear from me. My heart thudded. She explained that she was currently in Belgrade for the book fair that took place in the city every October but would be visiting her own parents (who I may remember had moved to the coast) in two days' time. Since I'd mentioned that we wanted to travel as far as Kotor, would we consider meeting her for lunch in Sveti Stefan on Sunday? There was now a good restaurant on the island.

Stefan? OK. How far is it? Luke said.

From Kotor? Forty minutes, I guessed. Less.

I was keen to delay.

Well . . . sure, I'm up for that if you are.

After a while we were directed onto the motorway. I prefer a straight road to avoid travel sickness, but also the certainty of it.

When we stopped for petrol, people asked me for directions, which at first seemed a good sign but then depressed me. Maybe our route was the same as when Daria and me had been going the other way. In the convoy of tourist buses commandeered for evacuations. Most of the passengers were unaccompanied children. A white UN truck like an egg carton had escorted us. When we got to Split there was a ferry waiting in the port.

Ancona, then England, then Glasgow. 1994, just after the World Cup, the summer the Channel Tunnel opened.

A woman who met us asked us if we were happy as I unwrapped her crayons from their skins. My sister translated. I had said no. Daria was embarrassed. Though everyone insisted it was not the case – that it had more to do with the cost of the tunnel passes and the need for men, the impossibility of abandoning their neighbours – my mother's decision to stay behind with the rest of my family, the suddenness of our departure in the middle of the night, the severance from our basement community, had felt more like exile than escaping.

I don't know what she told our basement family about me and Daria leaving, but the first time I came back, that gang of children seemed even closer to one another, and united in punishing those who'd left them.

Luke complained he was hungry. I said I might be able to eat something too now the nausea had subsided, but it was already three and most of the restaurants in the small seaside village we stopped in were closed.

Guess it's out of season, I said.

We found a bar still serving, though its umbrellas and terrace tables had been folded. Half the dishes on the menu were written in English, enclosed inside quotation marks.

I just feel like they'll turn out not to be what they claim, he told me, studying it.

He'd relaxed his pescatarianism since visiting his parents, so I ordered him what promised to be ćevapi (a skinless, garlicky sausage), a basket of bread and a Coke.

Thank you for driving, I said as the waiter retreated. And sorry, obviously.

What for?

For being sick. For blocking the sink.

Yes, that was quite shit.

Seeing me cringe, he laughed and leant in, kissing the skin below my eye.

That last bit was pretty white-knuckle. Good you were asleep. The drivers here are mental. Cliff one side, sheer drop – his hand sliced down – Adriatic the other, and the truck right in the middle of the road. On a bend.

The waiter returned and ceremoniously laid out cutlery and glasses. Luke thanked him at each stage of the ritual until he went, then asked me to teach him phrases (hello, thank you, goodnight, beer) and in some ways, it *was* like a holiday, because seeing things through his eyes (the karst mountains and pine forests, the shining path of the sun on the sea) made me feel as if I'd never been to the region and had simply read a crude entry in a Lonely Planet guide.

He had claimed his main reason for wanting to visit Dubrovnik was that it was a World Heritage Site. I knew what he meant was that the medieval walled city was used as a location in Game of Thrones. Saying he might watch an episode of GOT, as opposed to one in the rotation of series we watched together, was a cue for me to entertain myself, preferably in a different part of the flat.

As we waited for the bill he asked me about our next destination and I reminded him I'd never been. Instead, I took his phone and read from Dubrovnik's Wikipedia entry.

In 1991, after the break-up of Yugoslavia ...

I paused, unwrapping a boiled sweet Luke had saved from the rental desk,

... Dubrovnik was besieged by Serbian and Montenegrin soldiers of the Yugoslav People's Army

I glided over the blue hyperlinks as if they were merely waves moving in and away on a shore.

Back in the car I asked Luke to open the windows which were child-locked, and the smell of the pine, the past, hit me full in the face.

5

We reached Dubrovnik at sunset. Its aura sunk beneath the roofs of the Old Town, rendering the limestone walls gold then pink then grey. We found the Airbnb easily enough, an apartment in the eaves of a neat, white building with notepads and water glasses arranged on each side of the bed. It was obvious real people did not live there. The man who met us with the keys seemed like an estate agent, indicating a plate of complimentary halva before leading us out onto the small roof terrace to hear the bells that were now chiming. First on one side, then the other, the rhythm of the second becoming tangled inside the first. The first light and quick, the second deeper and portentous. They looped and took after each other like swallows, then began to fade, slow and dissonant.

Luke showered first, emerging head-shrunk and sleek with his towel around his waist. He stood dripping onto the floor, browsing restaurant recommendations on his phone. I washed my hair, put on a single coat of brown mascara and the one nice dress I'd packed. Looking in the mirror, I saw my colour had returned. That dress gave me something approaching cleavage. I knew Luke liked it, or the way it split the white meat of my breasts so I gained the little V-shaped shadow.

I leant closer so that the fur along my jaw glowed beneath the spotlit mirror. I licked my lips. When I came out of the bathroom I tried to hide what I was thinking, but Luke pulled me onto the sofa with my wet hair on his chest. He stared into my face as if he'd asked a question. My response was to bite. Sometimes I need to sink my teeth. I was ravenous suddenly, but Luke said we would be late. That's how quickly it happens, the power shifts.

We ran down the stairs and onto the street, my hair still heavy with water, the complimentary shampoo not quite rinsed. There was a chill now, though earlier in the day autumn had felt inconceivable. The limestone paved the streets as well as the walls of buildings. Worn smooth, they shone in the lamp-light like trays of melting ice. The streets were fairly empty, and we held hands, following the blue dot.

Luke described my appetite that night as carnal. I ate a whole schnitzel, took food from his fork, pretending to *bite the hand that fed me*, and drank most of a bottle of red wine. I let him catch my foot, which was cold, under the table, wrap it in the stiff folds of his napkin, then feel his way along my leg. Not having my phone, I felt anxiety but also freedom.

We shared a tiramisu and he shoved in beside me. I thought: How did I doubt him? And then: Here we are. No longer he and I but us.

Luke was drunk, and the conversation became more word association. He insisted on paying the bill as if I would argue with him over it. My treat, he said.

That morning I'd had a crust of vomit in the corners of my mouth and then he'd let me snore in the car most of the way here. *My treat* went back to an earlier stage, before he became my benefactor.

I was an indigent student, *art historian*, he continued, slurring. I should let him get this. He might have added I had minimal self-respect, for I had little desire to break my bondage.

The funded PhD was part-time, and so I made some income transcribing audio, mainly for a medical company, which I could do from home, writing dissertations for one of those essay mills (of which both Luke and Christopher especially disapproved) and tutoring – which also made me ashamed. It meant travelling all over London and into people's homes, often seeing how very wealthy people lived and how I helped perpetuate that wealth by getting them into elite schools and universities, even winning them scholarships. Among the children I preferred were the ones who could not have afforded those places otherwise, usually first or second generation immigrants. It weighed on me that their parents were throwing all the money they had on private tutors. Of these, my youngest was working toward the seven-plus. Her family had recently arrived from Bulgaria. The father was a cardiologist and had moved the family to an apartment in a high-rise near Canary Wharf without ever having seen it. They seemed pleased that someone like me had ended up at such a prestigious British university. I was, they said, a good role model for their daughter.

It made me feel good about myself certainly, but I also liked that child. I admired the way she approached verbal reasoning. Such as: should parents and teachers treat boys and girls the same? Answer: no, because you would not hug and kiss your teacher and your parents should not be too strict.

She was the age I was when I found myself transplanted to Mosspark Primary, learning to recite poetry by Robert Burns. That was where my desire to study humanities came from, I used to say on those personal statements and funding applications where you were asked to explain such things. I could have talked more truthfully about what Mira had read to me in the basement, but instead I cited the first Burns poem I'd learned. The one he addresses to the mouse – whose home he's just destroyed with a plough.

Despite what I wrote, it had not affected me because of 'the power of language' (I had barely understood it) but due to a physical experience. As I read the line: *Thy wee-bit housie, too, in ruin!* I had my first experience of what I later understood to be vertigo. The room spun violently to the left. Panicked, I tried to move with it, or rather against it, hurling myself out of the small plastic chair and onto the floor of my new classroom. In shock at hitting the ground, I began to sob uncontrollably.

For a few years, I'd also earned money working at a bookshop, but this coincided with the online rating of the bookshop going down. It was clear, Christopher said, from some of the customer reviews, that I had been the cause. One simply read: the girl at the counter is elitist.

When the waiter came back with the card reader, Luke returned to his side of the table and handed over his card. I reached my hand across and he held it while the machine whirred, looking, I felt, at the ring.

Let's go, I said. Let's walk.

But walking took too long, and I started to feel the good mood draining. I ran ahead, pretending to be some-one free-spirited. By the time we reached our doorway and he'd fumbled with the key, which required pulling the handle toward you with exactly the right force, we'd separated again. I wasn't sure whose fault it was, whether I'd created the tension with my false gaiety or simply detected it and then tried to paint over it.

Upstairs, I undressed, the way I would alone, not willing to give up though not willing to take the lead. Sometimes I worried my body had grown too familiar to Luke, and that was another good reason to keep it from him – the laws of supply and demand. But after a moment of stillness, Luke stayed my hand, slipped from the edge of the bed to the floor at my feet, pulling my underwear to one side and lifting his tongue into me. To steady us, his other hand travelled behind my thighs. I leant against the wall, tipped my head back, raised a heel onto his shoulder.

He was never rough. I suppose he thought I was extremely fragile. I faked a climax every time, hardly even aware I was doing it. If I did think about it sometimes, remembering my only boyfriend at university, I felt frightened. As if there was a dark void I might fall into without warning. But when I opened my mouth just then, the shuddering sound was something different.

I looked down at the top of Luke's head. I put my hand on it to check that he was really there – my surroundings in the strange room now surreal. Far away from where the day had begun, the night spent on the bathroom tiles, the acid taste of bile. His head tilted so that his eyes met mine and I found the door to the place I usually only find as everything's ending. Normally that feeling means I start to back away, pretend I've already come so he'll move on and concentrate on finishing. This time I didn't. I couldn't stand any longer and moved around him, lowering myself onto the bed, unsure of how I wanted the next part to go. Something like this, like the music heard through the open window – this other, unmapped level of the game – would turn out to be illusory, or happen only once, which was the same thing really.

No, he said. Not that.

No, I repeated.

I lay back and felt myself shrink beneath him. The shine of his collarbone level with my eye. Bird-boned, the same dizzy lightness I'd had all day but good now, spreading.

Inside me, I commanded.

As he pushed inside I went through another door, and I found myself smiling at how fast it was happening, how easily, as if I'd expected it to be locked but in fact it was open. The room began to turn. Rippling like it was fabric. Not a void, but I felt hollowed out, so that I became the air in the room as well as both bodies in it. The feeling was of expansion, lines melting away rather than emptiness, like I would black out if I stopped thinking.

I reached my hand around his arm for its solidity, the stability of him generally, and again, from some deeply worn groove, the reflex for thought over annihilation.

But just as I pulled back, I felt his body respond, his chin turned in, lifting off a little so he could see into my face.

I love you, he said, you know that?

I'd woken up first. From the short coma that follows sex if you haven't had it for a long time. The thud of sleep like a rebound that comes before real sleep. Waking in confusion to a room with the lights on.

His arm was wrapped around me but I needed to pee. I lifted the arm and slid out from under then scuttled to the bathroom, breaking into a run. Though it was a half-level down from the bedroom and sound barely carried, I reached forward and ran the tap out of habit. I towelled the insides of my legs, brushed my teeth, removed the smudges of brown mascara under each red eye. Staring at the face above the sink, thoughts returned to me. Like: I'd missed my pill that day. The previous day's was likely purged in the sink at home.

Fuck, I said to the mirror. *Fuck*.

When I woke again just before dawn, the room was dark but for a blade of light which marked the doorway and a blue line at the bottom of the windowpane. I'd been having a complicated dream and my first thought was to write it down as I usually do, to separate it from reality. Then I remembered the black rectangle that signified the missing notebook. I groped for the complimentary pad beside the bed and felt my way outside the room, closed the door gently and turned on the light, writing up the main points of the dream while standing naked in the display kitchen, pad pressed against the wall, until Luke gave a moo of irritation.

Back beside him, I couldn't sleep. My brain had returned to its fractious state.

It's the rich food, he said sleepily. We ate too late.

I thought of Luke's blood sausages and potatoes fried in oil.

I lay there and pretended to be sleeping but then a repulsive memory surfaced. The memory of my mother in a strange bedroom I'd been put to sleep in when I saw, through the slits of my eyes, her climbing astride a man – my father? – him pushing her away.

In the morning he sat half-dressed, the same corner from where he'd watched me undress the night before, now searching for a pharmacy. I paced the room then went to the fridge and ate both pieces of halva. He called out an address.

What time does it open? I called back.

Oh, wait, no. Ignore that. This one's old . . . Like a seven-hundred-year-old-apothecary. But we could go there? After. Might be fun? *Europe's third-oldest working pharmacy* . . .

At the counter I spoke in English. In case the pharmacist turned out to be religious I thought it would be better to feign ignorance. He looked confused. I took out the Airbnb pad.

Woah, Luke said, woah, woah. What're you going to draw this time?

I ignored him, forging a condom in one smooth line, then adding a jagged one to indicate a split, then a dashed, determined one, heading toward a circle. I crossed through the dashed line with a flourish.

Noli me tangere.

The pharmacist's posture stiffened but he went into a back room and returned with a silver packet of Escapelle, putting it straight into a bag for me. Luke handed over 200 kuna from a plastic wallet and then we turned, mission accomplished, pushed the door and walked briskly toward the steps of St Blaise.

While I sat on the top step and waited, Luke went to buy a bottle of water. I opened the box and toyed with the contents – a silver spaceship-like dish in which a single white pill had been sealed as though it might itself grow into an alien baby. My hands itched, I realised, for my phone. I toyed with the blister package.

I wondered if Christopher would be worried about me. Though I'd only been without it for twenty-four hours, this was perhaps the longest we'd gone without some form of contact in several years. In many ways I already had a husband, the kind Luke would never be, and I wanted to tell him about the previous night. The possibilities it had suggested.

Sitting on the church step, waiting for Luke to return, I relived the moment we first met:

After the ceremony. The glare of white stone. Us sitting on the wide, shallow steps leading to the church. The square before it a relief after the alleyways, dead ends and sudden drops. Neither of us really knew anyone. I had been struggling, feeling low in confidence, and we were waiting on the edge of a gang of braying family friends for the last boat in a wedding flotilla. No cars meant we'd started out even, at least in that regard. Neither of us knew it was bad luck to go to Venice together before marrying. I don't know if it's the same if you meet there.

When the boat arrived, a boarding school clique in damp linen suits crushed together. There wasn't room for the last four of us so Luke hung back. The other couple said they'd had too much sun anyway and would see us at the reception. We sat on the edge, spray from the Adriatic against our legs, looking at the deepening green of tide bands on the stone beneath us. The step's heat seared through the silk of my dress. I cast it in a circle around me. When he asked where I was staying, I laughed and said the cheapest hotel from the 'cheap' section on the website. That was our first joke. The wedding website. The *cheap* section. It kept us going in the early weeks, evolving quickly into shorthand. When something was unreasonably expensive it was *from the cheap section*, and when something that was supposed to be simple (like planning where to meet) got over-complicated, that thing got its own website. I did not realise then that he had his own flat his parents bought him. Luke did not think of himself as wealthy because he had some working-class relatives. His dad was self-made as he often told me. Besides, he was not a banker and had gone to his boarding school on a scholarship.

Later we saw the seating plan had us together again. Diagonally across on one of the long tables under strings of orange paper lanterns. As the sky turned green they glowed like sea creatures. A conga line started. Rowdy but affectionate Italians. I assumed Luke, who'd so far operated on the fringes, whispering savage commentary into my ear, would hold back, but he pulled me into it. Then, once our section came loose, I guessed the idea had been to reduce the intensity of our sudden pairing, to make ourselves available again to other people at the party. I thought we'd maybe circle each other awkwardly then lose each other half-intentionally on the dance floor. But soon I found myself hanging limp with my arms around his neck, both of us swaying gently.

In the boat going back from the reception, I watched how the dark, compact seaweed that hung from the walls of the buildings transformed in our wake, expanding, floating upward in bright clouds of green from the submerged brick, drunkenly convinced it was the perfect metaphor for our meeting.

The next day we nursed each other, eating only gelato. Hips pushing against the clicking turnstiles, my stomach fizzing and empty, head an ecstatic balloon. We tried to follow the blue dot but there was a delay, so following the map only sent us down wrong paths. There were no right ones it seemed anyway – everything was crooked and led back to the same square. I didn't care where we went, I said. Whatever he suggested was what I wanted. Pliable instinctively but also because the whole place was something to see, wasn't it? I'd studied its artefacts as a sixth-former but never in person. I hadn't understood, in the physical sense, that the city was stone on water, a sinking museum. I was mesmerised by the erosion of grandeur – monumental palazzos where the doorways had rotted and the rising water left the ground floors uninhabitable. To save battery, Luke had a book for learning Italian that had been free with a newspaper, evidently from years ago. It followed an English couple, Tom and Kate, around Italy, and referred to prices in lire. Tom worked *with computers* and Kate had been a teacher for three years but now worked for Rover. We quoted the lines they spoke to each other before painted altarpieces in dark churches. These were not the stock phrases I'd been expecting, but how a real, intimate couple would converse while navigating acqua alta. It was intoxicating, role-playing Kate, with her nice English boyfriend and middle-class tastes. I kept everything, every souvenir. All the tickets bearing reproductions of tiny details from paintings of heavy-lidded saints.

Noli me tangere, Luke read aloud, is the Latin version of the phrase spoken by Jesus to Mary – touch me not – when she recognised him after the resurrection. The original Greek is better translated as *stop clinging to me* or *stop holding on to me* – the attempt to stay joined together as an ongoing action rather than a single moment.

We stared at the returning Jesus, brushing away her outstretched arms.

At sunset we went to another island. I was keen to let him know I was reading Jan Morris. That I was considering a masters in Art History.

I started to tell him when we sat down. Talking fast, my eyes darting up to his face. Falling for him already. In those days my brain was always brimming with real things, facts, and I had to find ways to halt its progress for an audience. I found it so much easier to concentrate, to retain information. To use it to my advantage somehow. How the monks were expelled from their monastery by the Turks, then granted asylum on this island. How Venice was founded by refugees, forced to become seafarers. Half western, half eastern, half land, half sea.

On the morning we were due to fly home – separate airports, one expensive, one *cheap* – I'd woken to Luke's first disappearing act. From the open wardrobe, I heard the empty hangers sounding in the wind like church bells or far-off goats. I realised I was alone in the bed. I felt the damp air rising up the staircase and knew the door to the room was open. I aimed my gaze at the ceiling, lay still as if I'd been stabbed. The heavy yellow plaster sagged between the beams.

I got up and sat with my back in the sun on the small Venetian balcony. A couple, Italian, were arguing in a narrow street below, beside the canal. The woman was becoming hysterical. I leant over between the laundry lines and terracotta pots and saw them. The woman had sunk to her knees and the man was trying to pull her up. She seemed to be in shock. He tried to drag her along the street and she would not let him, but when he tried to walk away without her she screamed at him to come back. Finally, he gave up and walked away and around a corner so that she cried out again, louder. I'd closed the window, there was something about the scene, her helplessness, that had made me imagine her body, or the discovery of it, drowned. I remember thinking I would never let that be me, that woman and her body, her loud, inhuman screams.

Luke returned to the church steps holding a glass bottle and unscrewed it for me. I sliced into the silver foil and gulped the emergency pill down with ice-cold water.

6

Early on Sunday he went running. When he got back we drove from Dubrovnik to the Bay of Kotor, a place I knew I had once been to from a hazy memory augmented by photographs. The last holiday as a family, though we didn't know it then. Dan Republike. Daria, Drago and me sitting on an upturned fishing boat and beyond us the water, which I'd thought of as a lake but was actually an indented part of the sea.

Luke and I sat in a square with small glasses of bitter coffee. I wasn't in the mood for walking or looking at Venetian fortifications anymore and drew my fingernail back and forth along my chin. He took out his phone and started registering me with a company that specialised in locating personal property lost in international airports, asking for the details he needed in the same coaxing tone he used on animals he was trying to move.

The Escapelle had left me feeling unstable, or that was what I'd said, and I knew he was being kind to me because of this. After a short wander which made me worry we'd run out of things to say already, we drove on, arriving at the restaurant before Mira.

The hotel occupied the whole of the island, tethered to the beach by a narrow stone causeway. It had been a fishing village – simple stone buildings with red-tiled roofs, white shutters, cypress trees and pines set on top of the rocks. A woman at the reception desk escorted us along narrow cobbled lanes which climbed toward the centre and a table; the only one laid in an otherwise deserted courtyard presented to us as *the piazza*. Mira, the waitress said, had requested this specific table.

It was smarter than whatever I'd pictured. We scanned the menu, presented to us in English, Luke laughing at *forgotten vegetables* and deciding it must mean heirloom.

I like it, he added thoughtfully, looking around as if surprised. Here, I mean. Mira must be doing well for herself.

My head began to hurt – a sharp and insistent pain. I put one hand to my temple.

What does she look like? Mira.

Most of my childhood memories had her in them. I searched for her adult face and found it at the funeral; the doll eyes dead, face white and wet, but even then Mira was beautiful. Her face was like the Fornasetti woman's. She was the type Luke found most attractive. Dark hair, thin arms, oval face, no make-up.

On an early date, I'd asked him about his type and he'd claimed he didn't know or didn't have one. I'd pressed harder and he'd said: just not an English rose I guess. Foreign-looking, that was his thing. He looked at me as he said it, shrugging. My infiltration of his browsing history contradicted this.

As we waited I felt increasingly nervous, as if someone might be playing a massive trick on me, my headache getting steadily worse. I got up to pace around, saying I wanted to look at the view from the other side of the square, away from the shore, and found a tiny chapel tucked away there.

What about here for the wedding? Luke was suddenly behind.

I didn't turn around. I doubted he was serious anyway. The way he'd said *here*, I decided, was as if he'd used quotation marks. Since Cornwall, we'd not mentioned weddings.

A woman's voice could be heard talking animatedly and we returned to the table. Mira was there smoking, seated in the only chair not in full shade. She wore dark trousers and a black sleeveless tunic so that her bare, brown shoulders were flecked with sunlight beneath the trees. She turned to us, smiling, stubbing her cigarette in the ashtray as she rose to her feet. Slowly she came toward me and gripped both my wrists, staring at me with her large eyes for a moment, then pulling me in to her chest and whispering things I couldn't entirely make out so close to my ear.

It's lovely here, she said, reverting to the English of our emails as she shook hands with Luke.

It was jarring when she first did this, a betrayal of our former closeness somehow.

And you have to imagine Tito's poodles trotting around.

He laughed.

Yes, she said seriously, nodding as she lit another cigarette. He came here. Lots. And now they've made it smart again. It's very popular for weddings. Djokovic, you know the tennis guy? He got married here. Oh!

She spread her hands to where we sat on either side of her – I must give you my congratulations!

This was the first time anybody had said this and I hadn't felt like I'd been caught out in a lie. But I felt another kind of guilt. She wore large, chic rings on most fingers but Daria had never mentioned Mira getting married.

Luke pursed his lips and rounded his shoulders in a self-effacing way, looking from Mira to the table.

Did this belong to him then, this island?

She gestured behind her in the direction of the beach. That was his summer palace.

Not bad for a communist.

The waiter came and stood rocking on his heels to list the dishes of the day. Mira asked for a bottle of wine by name, without deferring to Luke as I usually did, then removed a pair of angular black glasses from her bag and began to read with great attention. With the glasses on she looked older and I realised she must be thirty-six or -seven now, if I was thirty-one. The age my mother was when the war started.

She told us her father had briefly worked on the island after Tito turned it into a hotel. That hotel predated this one, she explained, but it had, many years ago, been full of Hollywood stars.

Then, of course . . .

She made a swooping motion with her cigarette to suggest a steep decline.

He was an assistant to the manager, I think. That's why I like coming here. When he went back to Montenegro with my mother, ten years ago now? No. More. It was just when the owners had leased the island and were having it restored. He's pleased with the refurbishment I think, though he can't afford to come. They've redone the rooms inside, or made under, as you say, very monastic, much more basic than they were before and so naturally more expensive, but outside all the details are the same.

I looked at Luke, who looked at Mira with rapt attention.

I worked in a hotel once, she added. A horrible one in Belgrade, when I first moved there. I worked nights. On reception. Not for long. They fired me after I placed a wake-up call to the wrong room. I remember the man answering in a panic and apologising for having been asleep. Then of course he came to and was very angry with me. I've never been good at them, she laughed, wake-up calls.

The waiter returned. Mira asked if we would like her to order for the table and we agreed. It was exhilarating to see Luke's usual dominance checked as she pointed out antipasti and several mains. My headache was subsiding.

I remembered, she whispered with a confiding smile, still speaking in our language. No tomatoes.

I was moved by this, but also embarrassed that she could still recall the tinned pineapple incident. Whenever my aunt told me to think of children still in basements dreaming of tomatoes or cultivating them on balconies, keeping me at the table until every last one had been eaten, I would think of Mira. Having logged so many hours slumped in my chair after my cousins had left the room – trying to think of good places to dispose of them – tomatoes, then all fruit, became the manifestation of my survivor guilt. To avoid tomatoes, which felt childish, I now claimed to be allergic to nightshades, but then I had to be devious about potatoes, which I love.

The waiter returned with the wine and another came with fancy varieties of bread. Mira poured the oil into a dish then added an apostrophe of balsamic to it. It floated for a second, held in tension, before settling as a black dot on the bottom. Everything she did was mesmerising, and I saw Luke grow less reserved. It suddenly reminded me of spending time with her and my brother.

He asked her about Belgrade.

The book fair's where I've just been.

She smoothed her smart black clothes.

It's always stressful there, but this year . . . she exhaled . . . more so. I wanted to get out of the city and come here, see my parents, you know.

There was a long silence. Mira pressed her bread into the oil and the black dot exploded.

This year's fair had been decisive for her professionally, she explained, as well as significant in her personal life. One of her authors, a journalist she represented, had written a fictionalised account of the war drawing heavily on her own experiences. Many of the pages dealt with a man whom foreigners knew as the *butcher of Bosnia*. She'd give us a copy if we wanted, there were dozens in the boot of her car.

I felt Luke's arousal at the mention. A year ago we'd listened to a series called 'Most Wanted' which had featured a few crimes from my part of the world.

Mira fell silent again, chewing her bread with concentration.

Is he the, er . . . the one they found guilty in The Hague?

She continued to chew, her gaze steady on Luke.

Was that last year? He posed as the therapist? Or he was one, first, but then . . . The new age healer, I mean, or – no . . .

He trailed off, self-conscious again.

You've read the Edna O'Brien?

He's seen *The Hunting Party*.

She looked blank.

With Richard Gere and Jesse Eisenberg.

Oh. Well, you're thinking of the other butcher. Incidentally that one, the one you mention, yes, he posed as a healer, with his own well-being website and everything as you say, but he was also a poet. She inhaled deeply, reaching for another cigarette.

Karadick! Luke shouted, startling us, his spit landing on my cheek. That's it. I remember reading about him in the *Guardian*.

I shut my eyes. The evening before our flight, I'd found him watching a YouTube film set to Max Richter's 'Sarajevo', the same, trance-like expression he got listening to 'My Favourite Murder'.

Karadžić, I corrected.

He came from here, Mira said gently. From Montenegro. He only moved to Sarajevo in his teens. There was a lot of snobbery about him in the city. They dismissed him as a nutty peasant from the hills.

She gave a dry laugh.

A sheep-fucker, my father used to call him. People said he turned up in the city wearing pointy peasant shoes.

I had heard this from my parents too. Kulturni versus nekulturni. It was one of the few elements of their early conversations about the war I'd understood and absorbed – that this man did not come from a city, and that made him somehow less threatening to us.

Mira looked over my head toward two hotel staff members and back to us before lowering her voice.

It was Belgrade writers, literary, academic types, who came up with the ideological underpinning for what he did, Mira continued. And even when he was one of the most wanted men *in the world*, he published his novel and it sold at the fair in Belgrade! That was before my time, of course. I came the year they finally caught him. By then he was writing under his guru name, with a monthly column for *Healthy Living*. Promoting vitamins, crystals, and cleansing *auras* rather than whole villages.

But anyway. The other one, the other butcher – she looked around again – they haven't sentenced yet. They expect to next month I think. That's another reason it's all so fraught right now . . . the conclusion of the Mladić trial, the publication of the book . . .

She sighed and folded the fabric of her napkin into a rectangle, then a square.

I've had threats at the office. My home address has been put online. It's not out yet, the book, but I've had things sent to me. Awful, disgusting things. My mother had her email broken into, which she doesn't ever use so there wasn't much to find in there, but they sent out a load of messages pretending to be her, denouncing me. For a moment . . .

She broke off, raising her eyes to the swaying canopy overhead as the wind picked up, brushing her hair away from her eyes.

Well, I thought the email from you was something to do with it. That morning my assistant rang to say we'd had another phone call calling me a traitor.

Luke was shaking his head, and I reached out and placed my hand very delicately on hers.

But what are *you* being targeted for? he asked.

Oh, she exclaimed, brightening, for doing my job!

She held up her wine and tapped the glass.

For representing a very talented, very brave young woman.

She tapped again.

For defending her against the trolls who still believe it's an international conspiracy!

Then blinking hard, as if to correct her vision, she put the glass down and pressed her fingers into the table, nodding slowly to herself.

On the tram, when I got your email, I got this creeping feeling. I had this very real sensation, this hallucination almost, just as the phone buzzed in my hand, that a bullet or shrapnel or whatever had come whizzing into the back of me. I even put my hand there, on my neck. It was like I could feel something hot, like I'd been bitten.

She shuddered and took up her wine again, extracted another cigarette from a new pack.

I'm sorry, I said.

Don't be, she looked at me, switching out of English, it's so good to see you.

Both of you, she switched back again, rending the intimacy between us. Here. Nothing could be bad. It's only . . . a shame, that's all. To still be stuck talking about this. Even some of the publishing people I know say we should move on, stop making art about it, they say we're in paralysis, which is true, politically, economically, everything. That the worst books coming out of the Balkans are the ones still going on about war. They're as bad as the old stories, the folklore, which makes war seem inevitable. But it seems impossible not to talk about it when these people, these revisionists, still exist, even if we'd prefer to forget it.

The food arrived. Conversation turned to her non-work life in Belgrade. She had a nice life there, she said, a new apartment, nice new friends. I wanted to ask whether she still saw the old ones – the ones from our building, all adults now – and did they still call one another *comrade*?

She told us that until recently she'd shared a flat with a not-so-nice boyfriend, but thankfully he was not around anymore.

My stuff's only just come out of storage again. I wore this uniform every day at the fair, pretty much, because right now everything is everywhere – except for what I *need*, which is nowhere.

She laughed.

I just want to throw it all out and start again, really. It's not until you clear out rooms you've lived in for a number of years that you start thinking about – or begin to come to terms with – *how* you've been living, you know? In what filth and confusion, in my case. How did I function with all this *stuff* everywhere? And beyond that, you think about the choices you made – when? How did it all get here? Greed? Distraction? Did I carry it back bit by bit or did others bring things for me? Either way I want to be rid of it. Even my books mostly. I'm done with them. I need a change.

She flicked her hand as if knocking something off a shelf and into oblivion.

The world just becomes this mystifying accumulation when you start seeing things that way. Of people and street names and, like, all these buildings and political parties and front doors and plastic cones, all these posters that are ripped down and then pasted over. Putin, by the way, stares at me from every billboard in Belgrade right now. There's one eye level with my kitchen. Everything razed and then repaved, so that after a while you don't even recognise where you are anymore. But someone must know! Who is putting all these things everywhere in the first place and where, in the end, does it *go*?

Mira turned and signalled to the waiter. Luke widened his eyes at me and made a gesture against his nose, which seemed to mean *is she on coke?* I ignored him and returned my gaze to Mira, fixing it there, willing her to go on.

The other day I was sitting on my old sofa in the new apartment when I felt something sharp, sticking up through my tights. Guess what! It was Andrej's – my ex – his toenail poking right into my thigh. This thick, calcium . . . what's the word?

She made a motion like the Grim Reaper.

Scythe, Luke supplied.

That's it. I thought about putting it in a little clear bag, you know? Like with evidence from a crime, and sending it back to him with all the other things I keep finding that aren't mine. Whenever I change my sheets, I find little curls of his fucking hair. Woven into the duvet I mean. From his body. Not even his head. They've got themselves into the static. I thought to myself: for fuck's sake, get out! And I set about unpicking them until I started to get a pain in my neck from crouching over like some old spinster. I always say I'll stop and finish another time, but the task is never finished. I should keep them all and make some kind of quilt. Did you see the tapestry in Kotor? A medieval woman made it with her hair for her lover who was at sea.

She looked up at the trees for a while.

I think I'd like to be at sea maybe.

The waiter arrived with more wine and poured two large glasses for me and Mira. Luke put a hand over his.

It sounds like you're better off without him, I said.

Mira rolled her eyes. That's why I hate breaking up. It reduces everything to this single, frozen moment when it ended, and everyone picks sides depending on the version of history they heard first and who told them.

A young couple emerged from one corner of the piazza, holding on to each other in a way that suggested they were on honeymoon. Mira watched them and took out another cigarette, then offered the pack to each of us. Luke declined. I declined, then accepted, letting her put it to her mouth and light it first.

How come you broke up? I asked as I took my first drag, feeling an immediate rush.

Luke looked around then abruptly left the table. I assumed to find a bathroom, but there was something about his gait that made me watch his back as it retreated.

I couldn't sleep, Mira finally answered. I had this techno track going around in my head all night. It was driving me mad. I don't even know who it's by or what it's called, so I can't listen to it and scratch the itch, so to speak. There's no lyrics, so how could I find it? It's literally stuck in my head. And then, when I couldn't bear the broken record anymore, I'd switch to rearranging the furniture in the flat, mentally, imagining Andrej had moved out and I could put things wherever I liked with all the new space he'd left. Then when I couldn't rearrange the mental furniture anymore, I'd switch to the techno again. It fried my brain.

I haven't had that, she hesitated, since . . .

And I knew before she said it that she meant since Drago died.

She blew smoke up into the air and I felt the wine tip a scale in my head, the smoke clouding, something dilating.

After he'd died I'd had dreams in which he hadn't, in which I couldn't understand where I'd got that macabre idea, had worried there must be something wrong with me. That's when I started recording my dreams.

I hate giving up, Mira continued, so it took ages, and after I ended it I kept going back. Then that cycle . . . I just went back and forth in these figures of eight when I lay in bed at night with him snoring, weighing things up again, subtracting, starting over as if I'd missed a decimal somewhere. But each train of thought came right back to where I started. I tried massage, yoga, acupuncture. All to get rid of this compulsive self-narration I can't help. The dissociation – do you get that? And I did lie there and try to think about where my pelvis was poised in space – but in the end I decided the only solution was to explode it, otherwise I was going to spend my life that way, missing my exit, my opportunity to escape. So, here we are. Thirty-six. Single. Great.

Luke had been gone a long time. I remembered the weekend we'd memorised each other's numbers in case of emergency. But I couldn't remember the number now, only the fear.

With my friends I found myself defending him, Mira continued softly. They'd give their pseudo-psychological diagnoses. Then I'd be with him, we'd argue, inevitably, and I'd find myself agreeing with my friends.

Luke came slowly back toward the table, looking warily from Mira to me. The sky was darkening as if for rain.

You must be tired from driving, she told him. I only want a coffee but you two should try something, they have an excellent pastry chef.

She insisted on paying for the meal, since we'd driven out of our way to see her, and then, once she'd paid, suggested in her irresistible way we come with her after to her parents'. They would be overjoyed to see me, she said. Surely Luke would not want to drive all the way so late. The roads, as he must know by now, were lethal and it would get properly dark very soon. It wasn't an easy drive by day. He must've noticed not many companies would insure us. Why not spend the night in the upstairs apartment her parents kept for holiday lets?

I wished I could sound this self-assured when I wanted Luke to stay with me. He looked too tired to argue anyway and I was eager to further delay the drive. I called my sister from Mira's phone to tell her we'd now be there by tomorrow evening, not tonight. I could hear her daughter crying in the background which always took me by surprise – I had a niece.

Fine, was all she said.

7

The sun was setting as we tailed Mira. Luke pointed out the horizon of motionless cranes. Most buildings seemed to be under construction or arrested construction. Unclad, unfinished storeys of brick and concrete balconies without railings, already trailing black vines. Every other yard was littered with mounds of soil and sand, blocks of concrete, pallets, rubber coils, and every so often an old woman stood still as a statue among them, as if lost in her own front garden.

Spooky, he said.

What is?

This mania for building. With no one really here and nothing finished. It's like some great sickness hit.

We parked and stood waiting for Mira, who was reorganising items in her boot. The sky had turned a queasy orange, too warm for October.

It's like last week, I said to Luke. Do you think it's the same thing?

The week before we'd flown to Split, people stopped in the street and took photos of the sky. Storm Ophelia had brought dust from the Sahara and smoke from European wildfires. The sun was an apocalyptic red. The news reported birds swirling mysteriously. In Lancashire, where Michael's family came from, an entire town was covered in foam. In Cornwall, Anne told us, there had been beach invasions by Portuguese man-o'-war – also known as *floating terrors*. They looked like blue plastic bags on the sand, sometimes pink or orange. Rather than propelling themselves, they used their gas-filled bladders as sails. The high winds had blown them out of the water.

Extremely poisonous, Anne had captioned the photo she sent to their family thread. *Can't walk the dog!*

In Scotland, aged nine or ten, I remember taking part in a disaster relief mission on a beach somewhere when all the children came together on the sand to save a swarm of stranded jellyfish. A teenage boy, who did not help but stood around and watched as we dug a channel to the sea, told us in poetic terms all the information he had somehow learned about them. These milky, almost invisible creatures had no bones, no heart, no brain. They were 98% water in fact. This kind couldn't even pulse. They were at the mercy of the ocean, or they were the ocean, depending on how you looked at it.

Up until that moment I'd been taking part in the rescue mainly because of the sense of occasion, the urgent solidarity among the children. I hated jellyfish, ranking them alongside wasps, maybe worse for being inconspicuous. I'd imagined their sting to be vindictive – less a defence mechanism than a calculated marking of territory where happy children dared to swim. But listening to that boy, I'd felt my animosity draining. In that moment they were the most vulnerable creatures I could think of, entrusting their lives to total uncertainty in exchange for locomotion, moving wherever the moon, the wind, the water drove them. Venom was their one protection, the only thing they could control.

Luke studied the orange colour of the sky for a long time without responding to my question. Then, as we walked from the car park, Mira explained to him that construction work was not allowed in high season. It was all condensed into these months, when there was often bad weather.

The other thing, she said, letting Luke take her heaviest bag, is if they don't finish they don't have to pay tax. There's a whole Russian village up on that hill, completely empty. They just build these fake castles then leave off the roof.

We took back alleys, ducking under washing lines heavy with carpets and towels, before coming to a yard.

One wall had been sprayed with two words. FUCK LOGIC. In English.

This is the back entrance, Mira said. Safer. In case we're being followed.

She guided us past an improvised trellis with the fruitless remains of a vine.

Then again, as my friend Neda says, safety is a trap!

She laughed to herself and began coughing, a hacking smoker's cough, guiding us between two leopard-print towels and a number of real pelts, strung up beside her parents' door. Her father liked to hunt, she said. Luke would have to excuse them as their English was limited.

He stooped nervously in the low-ceilinged kitchen while the rest of us embraced. They'd aged since the funeral but said I had not changed. We sat at the yellow Formica table where the two of them had been eating, and Mira's mother passed black plums round with a bottle of slivovitz – the plum brandy, which, unlike the fruit, I liked.

Her father wore a green gilet with a hospital logo, though in my memory he'd worked for a tobacco company. He talked about moving to Montenegro partly because of more religious people who'd come to Sarajevo. They were more traditional, not socialist, he said. They feel about Erdoğan the way Serbs do about Putin. Like he's looking out for them.

They took the jobs too, his wife added before Mira chided her.

It's all changing.

But not enough, Mira said.

There are now new shopping malls everywhere, he continued. Shopping, only shopping. Like America.

You're obsessed with America, she groaned.

We discussed Trump, the pro-Trump fake-news sites set up by Balkan teenagers as a way of making money, and then Croatia's rising nationalism, with the opposite nostalgia in Sarajevo. When he asked how my father was I said it sounded like he spent most of his time, when he wasn't looking after my mother, in a Tito-themed cafe. He said he knew the one. Near that ICAR statue they had erected. A monument to canned beef with a little EU flag – an ironic gesture by the Bosnians to show their gratitude for what the international community had done for them during the siege. I looked at Luke, wanting to explain the joke in English, but I saw that he was looking at his phone.

Mira began helping her mother make a stew she told us we could have later if we got hungry, slicing mushrooms against her thumb, a motion which made me wince but somehow compelled me to watch her too, then she excused herself. A few moments later, from the hall, there was a strangled sound and then a cry.

I wondered if one of us should leave the table and go to her, but her parents sat still, as if nothing out of the ordinary was happening.

When she returned, her eyes were watery and unfocused, her hands shaking as she lit a cigarette. She spoke so fast I barely caught what was being said. Luke looked from me to her, as she paced the tiny kitchen before sliding to the floor and weeping as freely as if her tears were laughter.

I think, I said quietly, leaning my head toward his, Mira's author's dead.

Long after her parents went to bed, the three of us remained around the table. We sat there until my eyes were raw from smoke. Luke's became narrow slits, but he did not seem to want to go to the upstairs apartment unless I came with him, and I did not want to leave Mira.

It was unclear whether the journalist's death was a suicide or only staged as one. Mira was at first sure of the latter, but then went back and forth. I couldn't stop looking at her hands. They moved as if possessed, making it difficult to put the cigarettes between her lips.

Sometimes I wonder what good it actually does to *bear witness*, I remember her saying. That the whole world was fixated on us and all we got was Vietnam leftovers. Canned beef. We're supposed to be grateful they tuned in to watch?

At some point I got up to get some water and as I moved my vision blurred. I stayed a while at the sink to steady myself, letting my glass overflow, pouring it out, refilling, listening to the low murmur of Mira's monologue. Coming back, I saw a framed cross-stitch I remembered from their old apartment, which at the time I could not read. Now I saw it said, in English NO PLACE LIKE HOME.

I returned to my chair, turning these words over like I'd never heard them before in my life. Mira was telling Luke, now sunk deep into the sofa, why she'd really left Sarajevo. Ash flaked from her cigarette. I felt my eyelids shudder from the effort of keeping open.

They don't see a future, many of my old friends. I don't know what to say when I see them. I have this guilt, so now I try not to come back much. People like you though – she pointed her cigarette at me – I mean, I guess if you left as a kid, watched it on TV and not in person, only came back every couple of years, then everything reminds you of it.

This stung. I didn't say anything. It was true. But I'd been thinking how much this evening reminded me of being together with the others in our old basement.

The last time I went there was winter and the air was so toxic I could barely leave the house. I know your parents won't leave – but Daria could. She has a baby.

I nodded silently.

My mother wants me to have one. She says we should be replenishing the population. They're just as nostalgic as yours by the way. It's a kind of collective psychosis. I'm always saying what about press censorship? What about gay people? What about Goli Otok?

Luke frowned and mumbled something. Mira didn't seem to require anything more from her audience; her eyes wouldn't focus and she carried on, her words unstoppable as if it might kill her to fall silent. I felt hot. Excruciatingly hot all of a sudden. I pinched my earlobe. Her eyes finally locked on me and her hands dropped to her lap, still at last, silent, shoulders limp, the frantic energy now spent.

I think of him constantly, she said.

In my dream, I woke in the back of my parents' car still under my duvet but now across my sister's lap, my brother in the front where my mother usually sat, my mother in the driver's seat. No Dad. She rarely drove after dark and claimed to have poor night vision. As it was pitch-black on the road, I assumed we were on a mission to find my father and shame one of his girlfriends. No one would say what was going on except that we were going to grandma's to sleep over. When I woke a war had started. Shots fired on a wedding party that had been waving flags after the referendum. I remember this shocked me most because it involved a wedding and I could not connect that idea with death.

Early the next morning we said sober goodbyes, and Mira promised to be in touch when she next came to London. We picked our way back through the ghostly fairground of cranes and abandoned diggers, a greenhouse with weeds pressing against the ceiling, plastic chairs and low-hanging laundry lines. Luke kept looking over his shoulder. He seemed more vigilant.

Christopher says if you have to have a difficult conversation, walking or driving works well. That is to say side by side, in motion with a changing view. Luke found it easier for any conversation. For our relationship in general, sitting face to face across a table induced a hostile charge. But as we drove inland, I felt a new tension between us. I stayed silent and kept my eyes on the landscape, devoid of people, where life had apparently stopped.

What did you think of Mira? I asked finally.

Interesting, he said after a long pause. Very interesting woman.

Interesting, I repeated. OK.

Forthright, he added. She had opinions. Seemed very sure of herself.

I said nothing this time.

Very direct. Not like this route you're taking.

We'd chosen a winding one to avoid the motorway the satnav kept insisting we join every few kilometres. Mira had told us there was an old road through the mountains, tracing with her red fingernail the line on Luke's satellite image. You'll just have to watch out for landmines, she deadpanned, pinching the screen and handing it back to him.

The old road lived up to its name, moving us back in time and becoming increasingly pockmarked, passing abandoned homes with cows that wandered in front of us, disappearing again into ruins whose remaining walls still bore anti-NATO graffiti. There were no other cars, and as the road climbed swiftly higher, white mist occasionally surrounded us, blotting out all visibility. The houses became fewer and further, their aspects more hermitic. Occasionally we'd spot a miserable-looking donkey or dog chained up, or a lone figure would appear at the window. I had the feeling they could see something we couldn't – invisible but right in front of us.

We carried on past them until, up ahead, I could see what looked like a stone in the road. Slowly I realised it was moving.

I shrieked. Something prehistoric maybe. It was a tortoise creeping across the tarmac. Luke swerved, just missing it. The road had abraded as we'd climbed and where the brown shell edged along, veins of scrubby grass grew from fissures. He whistled slowly.

No car's come this way in a while.

A dog chained to a dilapidated building began to bark and then a man came out and stared at us as we passed him.

Do you feel like we're not supposed to be here? I said quietly.

For fuck's sake Anya, how am I supposed to know? You're supposed to be navigating.

We carried on for several minutes in silence. I could see the pulse in his neck. I told myself he was in a mood because he'd missed his run, but soon something else, black shapes just visible beyond another band of mist, stretched out across the road ahead.

What are *they*?

I shook my head.

He slowed our speed to a crawl and I sat upright in my seat, gripping the door.

Several tyres were strewn across the middle of the road, rainwater collecting in their cavities.

He clenched his jaw but made no comment. I thought of asking whether he thought we should turn around then but I didn't want to be responsible for any resulting decision.

The car made a strange whine, weaving between the tyres until the road was clear again and we reached the next ridge where Luke sped up, clearly desperate for the journey to be over. I pulled up the other route on his phone again but the dot pulsed frantically on white, the markings of the map wiped clear.

No reception up here.

Great.

I think if –

Jesus Christ

I lurched forward in my seat with the force of the brake but managed not to scream this time. Luke shot out his arm, too late to stop me flying forward.

I was expecting another animal or strange object, but only a few metres ahead the road ended.

Just stopped and disappeared. It fell away into thin air.

Don't move, he said, his voice shaking.

I'd never heard him be afraid.

We sat in stillness for a few seconds. Then Luke turned the engine off and gently opened his door, as though trying not to wake something.

Look that way, don't look forward, he said.

He climbed very slowly out. I followed, terrified the car would roll, moving my eyes in spite of his warning from the chasm where the road vanished – to the stub that remained on the opposite side. There was no sound except a distant roar of the motorway miles below.

Safely back from the precipice, Luke put his hands through his hair.

Why the *fuck* didn't one of those village *idiots* say something?

Maybe they thought we knew what we were doing. Our plate's Croatian, remember?

Where was the fucking warning saying the road literally cracks up and falls away?

I guess the tyres were the warning.

He kicked a rock over the edge. It fell soundlessly.

Well I'm not going back that way. No chance. I don't want to see those bastards gawping at us again.

I saw his hands were trembling now, as well as his voice, whether with rage or fear I wasn't sure but it was certainly *emotion*.

There was a dirt track back there, self-control returning as if aware of what I'd been thinking, we'll see where that takes us.

He got back into the car carefully, reversed a little way to let me in, then drove too fast down the steep dirt track as the tunnel of branches whipped against my window.

8

We parked near the Latin Bridge and Luke sent a photo to his family thread of the stone marking Franz Ferdinand's assassination. The result of their driver taking the wrong turn, or the right turn according to the original route.

With Luke beside me now I saw everything in high definition. Like the time I'd put on my first pair of glasses and looked up at a tree. The scars on the facades stood out more, as did the darker patches where they had been rendered over. I saw his gaze rest on the pockmarks concentrated around most windows and so I noticed them again as if they were new.

He wanted to get presents, including for my parents, and we wandered through the narrow streets of the bazaar. *Pazite, Snajper!*

Luke pointed silently to the rusting sign turned fridge magnet, waiting for my translation.

Sniper, I said flatly.

Who's this for? I wanted to snap at him, amid rows of souvenirs outside a shop called NOSTALGIJA.

He eyed up a pepper pot made from shrapnel, then settled on a copper serving dish.

The call to prayer sounded. It was getting late. We returned to the car and drove up the steep hillside. I noticed I was sweating.

He asked me about the last time I'd seen them in person and I lied and said I couldn't recall. That was my mother's way of dealing with things she didn't want to discuss, but I could remember it perfectly. It had been a weekend visit after my niece Hana was born. While my sister slept, I'd taken her baby for a walk in Veliki Park. There were lots of women pushing prams, but I held Hana, about six months old, tightly to my chest, stopping on a bench. Her little hand caressed one of the rotating memorial cylinders that bear the names of children who died during the siege. I realised I was gripping her too tight. Protectively. She began writhing so I loosened my hold a little, but when I next looked down, I saw a leaf disappearing into the dark O of her throat. She must have plucked it from a low branch over my shoulder, and now she began to choke.

I held her upside down and beat her violently until it came loose. She started screaming and would not stop although I reassured her, and myself, this had been an act of love.

When we arrived in my parents' neighbourhood, Luke's expression was that of a child who realises he has followed the wrong figure in a crowd. He looked at me as if I was a stranger.

It hasn't aged well, I found myself saying. It's different from the Austro-Hungarian stuff.

What are you getting defensive about, brutalism?

It's supposed to be about collective living.

Relax, you're making me nervous.

Sorry. I'm sorry.

So, he rubbed his hands, Elena and Jusuf?

He said it once more under his breath as we stood waiting for someone to buzz us inside the building.

And she's a teacher?

Yes. Was.

I'd not told him she'd been sacked for teaching *Macbeth* to her class and setting them the task of writing a suicide note.

And your dad?

A writer.

Like books or?

Sort of . . . bits of journalism. For a local paper.

And your sister's name again?

Daria.

And her husband?

Boyfriend. He won't be there.

But his name?

I, I actually can't remember.

My sister answered and told us which floor to come up to. In the lift I took his hand and watched his face, half in shadow in the mirror, his expression set. But I'd noted his disorientation before he caught it. As the lift rumbled upward, smelling of stale smoke, I slid the ring on my finger around to hide the yellow diamond.

Hana answered the door. She wore a translucent nightgown like some gothic heroine, and a chalky substance on her skin that smelt medicinal. I bent to embrace her but she took a quick step back and held her palm up to stop me.

Chickenpox, she said with the dignity of someone terminally ill. I'm off school. Have you had it?

Oh. Yes.

Noli me tangere.

In that case, she submitted graciously, we can touch.

The calamine smell was overpowering. Luke looked on bemused, waiting for an explanation. Hana glanced at him shyly, then waved us both through and ran out of sight, leaving us standing in the small corridor.

She has chickenpox. You've had it right?

No, he said slowly. I don't think so.

Oh. Well this probably isn't the right time to be exposed to it.

I don't know. I'll ask my mum.

He retreated to the doorway and took out his phone. I studied what was visible of the apartment – I didn't know it but I also did.

The little ghost returned with a glass bowl of bright orange crisps in one hand and a bag of peanuts in the other.

This way, she said primly.

She wanted me to see a house she'd made for woodlice on the balcony, though all the lice must have recently escaped. Luke joined us and stood gazing at the view. The hills dotted with white tombstones.

It was a relief to me that we'd been met by Hana, who appeared to harbour no discernible resentment, though I'm sure Daria discussed her own antipathy toward me in front of her daughter.

How old are you, I asked, as she crouched down to shut the sliding door again behind us.

I'm six now. And three-quarters.

The sun was nearly gone and I began to feel cold. Luke had seated himself in a plastic chair and was still scanning the silhouette of the hills as the sky turned swiftly violet. Setting off the geraniums growing in the red slouchy boots that were actually terracotta pots. My father adored these – one of the few things we still had from the first flat. Or he might've bought a replica. I guess that makes more sense. I felt Luke throbbing beside me, as if he was about to go on stage.

Actually Hana, I'm a little cold can we go back inside now?

She took a crisp from the bowl as she led us back again, the white gown floating behind her. It had been my mother's, I now realised. I motioned to Luke to sit down.

She set the crisps down on the table. I noted her downy moustache and seeming unselfconsciousness. I thought of myself, two years older, on my first day at Mosspark. I'd spent hours that morning tugging at my fur with my fingernails, pulling it out in clumps. All I'd wanted was to be blonde and otherwise hairless with a name like Amy. While it was not that remarkable to encounter foreign surnames on a class register in Glasgow, mine glowed radioactive in the nineties. Certain teachers looked up from the list in horror – as if I myself was violently disintegrating.

And then, on that first day, I was one of two who couldn't make it to the top of the rope to ring the bell in Gym. Hearing the screams below to GO GO GO, I panicked. Unable to go on or to let go and fall to the mat, though the rope cut into my hands as I clung to it. Suspended there, halfway between the peeling paint of the ceiling where the brass bell hung and the baying mob below, I noticed new growth along my thighs. Gradually I understood what they were chanting in syllables. Hair-y An-ya. Hair-y An-ya. That night I got hold of my aunt's foul-smelling depilatory cream and nearly burned my skin off.

Mummy's helping Nena. Daddy's with Deda. Out.

She says Daria's helping my mother get dressed and my father's somewhere with her dad.

Luke eyed the little ghost warily as it offered him the bowl of crisps.

Tell them to get comfortable Hana, a voice – my sister's – called, then, switching to English, I'll be out soon.

By the time I left Sarajevo, I knew lots of English words already from school and subtitled films. Even during the siege when schools had closed, Daria would read to me from what books she still had, books that had not yet been used for fire.

When are you going to tell them? Luke muttered. He seemed unsure if Hana could understand him.

He'd been the one to suggest we do this in person rather than before we arrived. That's the kind of thing his parents cared about, along with thank you letters and other arcane formalities I'd come to excel at.

I'd wanted to do it in an email ahead of time. I'd written long ones, which I'd cut down to short ones, then hadn't sent. I knew we would have to do it on the first night, get it over with, and that then there would be the question of whether they would come, with the answer being that of course they would not.

Dinner, I replied.

Now Daria emerged. I noticed, with some satisfaction, that she'd gained a bit of weight. Her skin looked grey, her dark hair was scraped back from her face.

Zdravo, she nodded.

Turning to Luke: Hi.

Her eyes barely met mine, surveying me briskly and shaking Luke's hand, explaining my mother still wasn't ready to greet us. I was sure even Luke could pick up on it.

So, you found us. Eventually.

She had a way of making statements so that I sensed she was actively avoiding posing questions to me. Making a point of her lack of interest in my life, in case I mistook curiosity for envy.

Minus a near-death experience, Luke said, reddening as the words left his mouth.

Daria's eyebrows raised a fraction.

We'll eat at nine, if that's alright with you.

Of course, I said, we had burek half an hour ago.

Daria went toward – but not onto – the balcony and lit a cigarette. She did look much older. Our aunt had stuck her Bristol graduation picture to the fridge, saying she looked like Olivia Hussey. None of us had heard of her. But when she put on the VHS of Zeffirelli's *Romeo and Juliet*, her daughters and I were furious, though I was proud as well. I hadn't realised how beautiful Daria was until I saw her likeness on a screen. I have a similar thing when I look at photos of Luke. Without being there, without it being the real him, he looks completely perfect.

Mira says hi, I said, switching out of English for a moment to be conciliatory as I came toward where she was looking for an ashtray. It was nice for us to see her. Her parents send their love.

Hana arrived with glasses and a jug on a tray in the same style as the copper serving dish. I noticed Luke fiddling with the gift at his feet while we spoke our language. His eyes wandering again to the hills which were now blue, as though they'd moved further away into the distance.

She found the ashtray and opened the sliding door a crack.

What was the *near-death experience*?

Oh, a road fell away, or had fallen, and there was no warning put in place.

My sister snorted and Luke looked awkwardly around the cramped room.

Doesn't *feel* smaller, this apartment. You said –

It is, she shot back, flicking the ash so it blew inside. She nodded to the leather sofas crammed behind her. And the building has a communal laundry instead of each apartment having their own machine. You get electric shocks from it so we wear rubber shoes to go down. You can borrow mine if you need to do any washing while you're here. However long that is this time.

I ignored the non-question.

Thanks. Where do we sleep?

Goran and I are going to stay with his cousin.

Goran, that was it. It means man of the mountains.

OK, if that's OK with you.

My sister shrugged.

Hana poured out glasses of lukewarm water then sat between us, eating peanuts from her white hand.

How long's she had it? I asked.

She's not infectious anymore. It's crusted over.

I had to wear gloves before, Hana piped up proudly, so I couldn't scratch. But now I can use my fingers.

She wiggled them. I wiggled mine back, grateful for her presence if only as a buffer.

OK, I said, well that's good. Luke isn't sure if he's had it.

Luke? I switched to English, has your mum replied?

She hasn't, he said, looking up from his phone on the sofa. I don't think I've had it, but I'm sure it's fine. He smiled at my sister meekly. No problem.

Daria raised her eyebrows unmistakably this time. A voice called from inside and she excused herself.

That was the end of the universe, I said to Hana who had followed my gaze to the hills. Even now, I continued – surprised, feeling something like adrenaline coursing through me – when I see them, even though I *know* we just drove through them, it's like I'm looking at a photograph and there's nothing out there, beyond.

I glanced at her and she nodded.

Can you show me to the bathroom?

I followed where she pointed, the door open beside the one Daria had just shut. I pulled the cord for light and a fan came on. The walls were peach-pink and peeling. I sat on the side of the bath and took deep breaths. A framed picture hung on the wall above the towel rail. My mother holding me as a baby, taken in our old bathroom, in our old bath. Her smile blissful, eyes shining, the skin on her naked shoulder shining too, her body curving around mine. It was so bleached by sunlight it looked almost artfully overexposed.

My hangover was maybe kicking in again and my stomach made strange gurgling noises. I reminded myself I always got this sensation of dread when I'd been drinking. Daria knocked to tell me Mum was ready. Looking in the door's direction, I noticed strange marks in the painted plywood where the light caught them, like someone had once struggled to get out.

*

The living room, when I returned, looked even more crowded and was now lit by some unforgiving ceiling lights. The two identical sofas faced each other with a narrow strip of floor between, the width of an armchair sandwiched at one end. Luke looked claustrophobic. My mother was now sitting in the armchair between the two sofas. She also looked very small and boxed-in. Her face unfamiliar thanks to the way her hair had been clipped back, and new white teeth that appeared when she smiled. They were too big, making her face seem even more shrunken. Under her eye, a delicate swell like an aubergine. A faint crust at the corners of her mouth when she closed it. The teeth pushing against the skin stretched over them. She stared at me placidly. Luke sat beside her as if waiting for someone to take a photograph, Daria took a seat opposite him. As I leant in toward my mother I caught the smell that had so disturbed me the last time I'd visited.

Whether it was really Alzheimer's or something more in her control, it began before the siege. That's when Daria says she first noticed something. Nothing dramatic. She would repeat or forget small things. Clear away a cup of tea that my sister had just put down, then if asked why it was missing she'd insist angrily that she hadn't touched it. If she'd just brushed it off as something she'd done absent-mindedly, Daria said, I wouldn't have thought anything of it. But she was often aggressive, saying I was criticising her and making things up.

During the siege, such symptoms barely registered. Depression, apathy, paranoia . . . these made her seem sane. She developed a slight tremor in her hands and said she felt weak, and that too seemed entirely reasonable. Then, to my father's exasperation, she began to act out her dreams, often hitting him squarely in the face.

When the siege was over, my father told my aunt she'd begun to experience hallucinations and would often seem disoriented, but many of their neighbours were experiencing similar things. It wasn't until after Drago died that there was a noticeable decline, though again the symptoms were masked by what was happening. She was only in her mid-sixties but had finally been diagnosed a few years ago, right after she had a fall. It became harder to speak to her on the phone after that. I felt even more self-conscious and my calls seemed to make her more agitated.

She appeared to confuse Luke for Drago at first, rubbing his arm distractedly. Then, from the greetings Daria translated, she seemed to decide we were being visited by another foreign journalist.

She wants to know if you know Christiane Amanpour, Daria said. She thinks you work for CNN.

I stared at my sister in disbelief. For years, until Drago died, we avoided talking about the war – quickly tiring of the same bad news. After he died, it was never spoken of at all. Daria stared back as if to say yes, this is what we are dealing with now, what *I* am dealing with while *you* are not here.

Luke smiled nervously.

She's been stuck in a version of the siege since August, Daria explained. Dad's convinced it's best to go along with it.

Around the time I met Luke in Venice, Daria had persuaded our father to try a home. She was supposed to be safer there, but she hated sleeping alone in unfamiliar surroundings. In turn she became unrecognisable. He'd told me the doctor prescribed her antipsychotics. She could barely move her eyes while she was on them. I remember getting a call saying he'd taken her out again and devised his own system for her care.

The idea was to embrace the alteration, as Daria said, like putting on a play. Resisting or trying to reorient her only got all of us more lost. You couldn't persuade someone back into who they used to be if they were dead set on living in the past. To find her we had to enter her reality, he'd concluded, and meet her at whatever landmark she'd found.

War metaphors were banned. Mum was not *fighting* a disease, there was no winning or losing. Nothing was invading her or taking over. When we spoke after the 2016 presidential election, Dad said the new guy proved what he'd always said. We lived in a demented society and everything was coming apart, so why not embrace the fragments like the pebbles on a beach.

Some things, he conceded, were harder to play along with. Letting her believe she had to keep away from the window – where until recently she had liked to sit – seemed cruel, for example. But as a result of his methodology, she'd passed from a state of anxiety into one of occasional euphoria.

I did not have the same abilities with her as Daria or our father, switching between these multiple worlds. I felt neurotic when I did, and afterward it was I who needed consoling. I longed for her to hold me. For her old smell. It felt like another casting out, this change, even as my mother's look charged me with abandonment.

Instead Christopher soothed me. Making up for husband *and* family. He said it didn't matter whether she recognised me now because I still knew who *she* was. I didn't say that I was constantly looking for ways to erase this knowledge. Because her deterioration had accelerated exactly when we started dating, each time I saw Luke with his family the desire grew sharper to escape mine. To learn to stop wanting something from them it was now too late to get. I was afraid that if Luke ever met them he'd recoil. Feel the sudden vertigo I did watching my mother grapple with reality. Without telling him things I was ashamed of, complex things, I couldn't make him see that coming back was no homecoming for me. That I felt surer of my place there if I stayed away.

On my rare visits, I'd attempt to do practical things for her instead, cleaning her teeth or spooning her food, but I could see she found me threatening.

It reminded me of our first reunion but in reverse. I'd been nervous on the journey from Glasgow, but assumed the feeling in my stomach must be excitement. Then when I finally saw her, something froze. I couldn't speak. She went to hold me and I felt myself go limp. My eyes rolled back and away from her. I shut my lips, clenched my arms, and would not submit even though she begged me.

Later, if I was mired in my thesis or in a particularly vigilant mood, reading every unspoken message Luke sent me, I became terrified early onset dementia – out-of-mindedness – was happening to me too.

When memories from the past intruded (tunnels, basements, waiting for contact, certain foods) I would worry about it even more. Maybe they were not a sign of what I thought they were. I would focus on physical sensations of relief. The sun on my face. Finding a precarious spot to balance a glass in the curved slats of a bench, releasing my feet from their shoes or sitting when my feet were tired. Coming into the cool when I was hot, washing my hands when they were sticky, pressing my cheek into the sleeping heat of Luke's back.

Is it shelling? she asked Daria, the way you'd ask someone if there was rain.

Nope, all clear.

What network are you from? she said, sitting up and cocking her head at Luke suspiciously, American?

Reuters, Daria said quickly, passing him a pad and translating simultaneously. He's just going to write some notes, he wants to hear your point of view. Shit. I need someone to get a can of cream. You still can't drive?

No.

I'll go, Luke said.

No. Thank you. You stay here and talk with her. Entertain her. I'll ring Dad. He must be on his way back by now.

Listening to my mother speak then it was as though she was telling me a made-up story. The kind I'd once begged her to invent, not read from existing children's books. Then, in the middle of saying something, she stopped and looked straight at me. Not as though she was lost, but had detected something, like a cat padding along a path who suddenly freezes.

9

The first thing my father did after closing the front door was to pick up Luke's rucksack from the hall, walk gravely into the living room with it hanging from his index finger, and ask in a threatening manner if Luke knew that APC stood for Armoured Personnel Carrier.

At least that's how I translated it.

His sense of humour can be unnerving. In the last census before the war he'd circled his nationality as Pacific Islander. Apparently I'd scolded him. I was too young to remember – it sounds like me. Beating my puny fists against his shins from underneath the table.

Tell the truth Babo!

This *is* the truth Anja! His voice mimicking mine.

Stop being silly!

Babo's not silly, he protested, it's everyone else that's gone mad.

His jokes are not intended to make other people laugh so much as frighten or confound them, which makes him laugh. This tendency made his sublime tenderness toward my mother all the more surprising.

My father dropped the bag and his face creased into a smile. He was reassuringly the same compared to my mother. The very large hands and ears. I waited for him to address me individually.

Here's your cream, Daria.

Then looking around, What, can't this English guy take a joke?

No one translated but Luke offered him his hand.

Dad says it's good to meet an Englishman, I lied.

Thanks, Luke said, Well. Cornish technically. It's good to finally meet him, say.

Daria clicked her tongue as she got up to turn the oven on. I sat beside my father, opposite Hana and Luke, too close in a way that made it impossible to really look at or talk naturally to one another. My mother still in the central chair in the narrow gap, as if we sat around an open casket.

I had expected, I realised, the conversation to focus more on me, or at least *us* rather than Luke. I did do the majority of the talking. Filling in for him more than I usually did and having also the task of translation. He explained – then I explained – his job so that, at first, I managed to make him sound like a eugenicist before I tried again to explain bioscience.

The future is uncertain, I said, starting from the top.

My father nodded impatiently.

Crops get domesticated and can't adapt, so we need diverse seeds to survive climate change and other bad things we can't anticipate.

Before, I'd always applied these ideas about domestication to myself. The task of translating made me heed what he was saying in a more objective way, less encumbered by other interpretation. Hana seemed enraptured. My mother's mouth hung slightly open.

Do you know the story about Leningrad, Dad asked him, via me.

I said he knew about the siege.

Leningrad was the home of the greatest, most diverse as you call it, seed vault in the world. Nikolai Vavilov's. Stalin put him in a gulag. But his staff stayed at the vault, which became their safe house, though many of them actually died protecting the seeds. The curator of the rice collection starved at his desk surrounded by bags of rice.

He started cracking up at this idea before I'd finished translating.

In exchange for this anecdote, Luke described the vault they built in the Arctic circle. Though it was designed to be an impregnable deep freeze, it had barely been five minutes before rising temperatures caused the permafrost to melt and the entrance to the tunnel flooded. Both he and my father laughed at this.

People are in denial, Daria said. They are afraid of their own death, the end of civilisation.

The laughter ceased.

And what do you do, Daria? Luke asked.

I was about to translate again, forgetting Daria spoke perfect English.

What do I do?

She fixed her eyes on his as she spoke. She was using her lawyer voice. Hana looked from Luke to her mother, sensing danger.

I'm a mother, she said, eyes narrowing. And I clean the surgery.

She got up and excused herself.

Where's Daria gone? my mother cried suddenly. She hasn't gone outside?

She's just in the kitchen, making dinner, I reassured her. Hana, why don't you go and see if she needs help.

The high-rises all rely on electricity, my mother said, addressing Luke so I translated again.

The water is pumped, the lifts, everything. There wasn't a chimney. So we had to move into a place someone we knew abandoned.

I left the last part out.

You don't think much about how everything works under the surface until it's broken – you just rely on each thing to do its job. Then you can't keep clean, you can't wash anything, when food does get through we can't eat it. Pasta, rice . . . everything requires boiling and we have no water to do it with. No heat. No electricity. So then we moved in here with my mother. But my mother is no Chetnik, you understand. She was AFŽ.

That's like feminist Antifa, I added.

The war is only between nationalists and those who are not insane, my father said, rubbing her hand in his.

Luke seemed to be finding the polyphonic, repetitive conversation difficult. I too was starting to feel quite mad.

What about her mother?

He asks you how your mother is.

Well she's deaf now. Can't hear the shooting, which is nice. But she can see how our faces change when it starts. She says the last war wasn't as bad as this one. My father fought against the Ustaše also. Did you know Sontag came here?

Not here, I said, not to the flat.

Would you like another drink?

Yes, please. Thanks.

Hana, go on, get him one. And help your mother like I said.

Mother? My mother said.

Yes, my father said.

Well, she was suddenly fed up, Mother knows all about wars. She predicted it. The women in this family have the gift of foresight.

This time it was me who laughed.

Some of the things she says, I said to Luke, aren't memories. Or they're not her memories. They happened to other people, or they're threads from stuff she read as a child, not always real. But now all mixed up as if they happened to her.

An acrid smell was coming from the kitchen. My sister called out that dinner was ready.

As my father told each of us where to sit, I shifted my gaze between my mother, my sister and her daughter. Memory passing down generations like water seeping through a multi-storey building.

At the table, he pulled the same trick he played on every first-time guest. It had been a while since I'd witnessed it and had forgotten the set-up until I heard him say slyly that Luke should be served first. I clenched my fists as Daria placed a plate of spaghetti Bolognese on the checked blue tablecloth before him and Luke raised his fork tentatively, sensing something was off by the way everyone was quiet and either watching or studiously *not* watching him. He tapped it suspiciously, then grinned.

My father slapped his shoulder, roaring as if this had never happened before, announcing, as he raised his glass toward him, that Luke was *OK for an ecofascist*. The ritual over, Daria set down plates of real food, less appetising than the resin version. Overcooked white fish, boiled carrots and buns not quite thawed from the freezer. The smell turned out to be rice she'd burned while trying to reheat it. In the oven. Daria was always a sophisticated cook so she did this to embarrass me.

She sat not eating, her elbows on the table, chin resting in her hands, so you could not see her mouth. I chewed the fish politely and tried to make myself swallow it, noticing an ulcer right between the skin and my bottom row of teeth. Throughout the meal I kept probing it with my tongue even though it made it hurt more.

It was too much effort to continually translate banal bits of conversation, and I let a lot of it go over Luke's head.

So you had a look around, Daria finally said in English. Even Luke must have sensed her sarcasm.

Yes, the old part of the town is great, he replied uncertainly. And the new bits are nice too.

What else did you see, the genocide museum?

No, I said curtly.

Maybe next time. What about the tunnel? It's very popular with the Chinese.

Yeah, I'd like to see that, Luke said.

I'm sure you would.

What's that supposed to mean? I said, switching out of English.

We had enough of people like him at the time.

Don't do this now.

Don't what? Hana said.

What's going on, Darko?

Nothing, my sister said. Who wants dessert?

After Drago died and Daria returned, my father had affectionately started calling her Darko. A boy's name. He joked she could live as a viržina after he died – a sworn virgin – the old Balkan thing of allowing a daughter to live as a son. She could start dressing as a man, working outdoors, carrying a gun. The catch being a vow of celibacy.

Darko found herself a boyfriend but the name persists.

Clinton is the worst president we could have at a time like this, my mother said, back from somewhere else. He's like a president from a TV show.

Yes, Daria laughed, it's a shame.

Who's she, sitting there?

It's Anja. Don't you remember?

Sometimes it felt easier to hate my mother. Certainly less painful.

Oh yes, she said, a faint smile forming. Then her face fell and she pursed her lips.

It was hard to pretend after that and I kept my eyes on my plate as something black rose up inside me.

Daria watched me clear my end of the table before everyone else had finished eating.

You have weak wrists, she said, following me to the kitchen. You could never be a waitress.

She said she had wanted to do a dessert in my English boyfriend's honour, and returned to the table with an Eton mess. She had, she explained, given it a modern twist using some leftover food colouring in the cream.

Why green? I asked after a silence.

Experiment.

Then, to everyone else, in a more civil tone, At first, I only added a little, and actually too little is disconcerting, so then I added the whole thing.

When she did things like this I willed Daria to admit that she was bored.

How was Mira, my father asked. The first real question he had addressed to me. We miss her.

I noticed my mother sweeping the table with her palm. It was something I'd seen my grandmother do, and now my mother was doing it repetitively. When she noticed me looking, she stopped.

Happy in Belgrade, I said, then again in English.

I gave Luke a look I hope conveyed that he should not mention Mira's author.

But she was visiting her family, Daria muttered, I don't understand.

What, Daria? I sighed.

How can she be in another city and still find time to see her family?

I ignored her, turning instead to my mother. Mum, what about some chocolate?

No, Daria said, as she grabbed my mother's wrist, you don't get to do this, you can't waltz in and out whenever you like! I'm sure you think I'm a bad person, she continued, wresting the language back into English, and addressing herself to Luke. I don't know what she tells you, but it's lies.

Her voice was even and cold again, as if she'd been preparing this. I couldn't speak. Luke began breaking his meringue into smaller shards, as if this might defuse the situation. Hana and my parents waited for the translation.

We're getting married, I shouted.

My father looked astonished, and for a moment no one said anything.

We're getting married, I said more quietly in English.

His first question was whether I planned to take Luke's last name. I said I hadn't yet decided.

What's happening? Anja's getting married? When?

We don't know yet, I lied.

Don't look like that Anja, my father said. It's not your funeral. I thought marriage had died out though, I must say. Do people still have weddings?

Where's the ring? Hana demanded.

I don't know why women do it, for men it makes sense, Daria sniffed. They get unpaid domestic labour.

I unscrewed it from my finger so that I was left with a pale line, and gave the diamond to Hana who studied it. Then I took up a position at the sink, letting the hot water run to scalding. A cloud of steam rose, and still I held my hand under the column for as long as I could bear it, remembering when Daria and I got to Split and finally we had water, just running, running, running.

I put gloves on when the pain became too much. Inside gloves the heat and pressure were reassuring. Starting with the sharp things, moving mechanically on to the blunt, I let the oily water drain then ran the tap again, waiting for it to turn hot before realising – I'd used it all up.

From the table I could hear the conversation continuing without me. They had changed the subject from our engagement already.

If I'd directly asked for my father's opinion he would have told me that marriage was bourgeois. Only for women who wanted families. The family was also bourgeois. He should know. If I'd said I was actually doing it to escape, to make a bid for *freedom*, he would have said that this idea of freedom, which was Neoliberal freedom, was more bourgeois than the family and would prove to be just as stifling.

I wanted to see the photo in the bathroom again, as if that could confirm I'd once belonged with these people. I moved slowly and experimentally, as though each thing in my path were a tremendous obstacle.

I smiled exaggeratedly at Daria as I passed.

Hana's brushing her teeth, my sister said, you'll have to wait.

She got up, turned her back, went to the kitchen archway and calmly folded out the concertina doors behind so only her legs were visible. The overhead lights turned on. The candle flames bleached out. Things formerly outside the circle now emerged. The condensation on the windows, knives shining on the magnetic strip, a halo of needles around the potted cactus.

Tell Daria she mustn't go out or I'll kill her! Mum said.

You'll kill her? I heard my father repeat, I thought that's what you were worried about.

I worry whenever any of them go outside, she said to Luke. My eldest wants to study abroad and never come back.

This time I translated her faithfully. I was too tired to manage the situation any longer.

At least we have good views! A sly grin spread across her face and she waved her bony arm in the direction of the hills all around us.

All new windows since the shelling!

She laughed then broke into anguished, noisy sobs.

I sat in rigid silence with Luke while Dad shuffled her to bed and Daria put Hana to bed on the sofa, took her bag, and left.

Hana, with her mother gone, asked to watch a movie. My father sat in the armchair this time, and she wriggled between me and Luke with her feet tucked under mine. As the opening credits began she settled into a rhythm of gently rasping breaths.

I've watched *Home Alone* about ten hundred times.

So have I, I said.

I'd first watched it during the siege. It was the last VHS we bought before it started. I remember whenever the power came back on Drago would be watching it while rewinding another one with a fork. Then it was a Christmas ritual at my aunt's in Glasgow, but I'd never found it very comforting. Her kids identified with the boy's struggle to defend his home against the forces of destruction, whereas I could only think about the trauma of being left behind.

It was even worse watching it as an adult. Or watching Hana laugh maniacally as the invaders were repeatedly foiled. I felt myself leaving my body. Floating up toward the ceiling, into another atmosphere where sound did not carry. From there, looking down at the child in the white nightgown, I experienced that version of loss which is a casting out of subject rather than an object.

*

In Hana's narrow bed, Luke turned the lamp off and stars appeared faintly on the ceiling, adding to my sensation of floating outward into space. We lay in silence for a few minutes.

I want to go home, I said.

I knew he was awake but he did not respond. After several minutes, the glow of his phone. The nimbus around his back.

Serious question, I said.

What?

Nothing.

What?

Do you still love me?

What kind of question is that?

He removed his leg from where it brushed the edges of my body – so that no part of us was touching anymore.

I can't sleep.

Well me neither Anya.

It struck me then why it is that the English phrase – *to drive home* – means to make someone understand.

In the middle of the night I could no longer bear it and insisted that we leave without saying goodbye. We would check into a hotel before tomorrow's flight. I could not spend another second in that place without imploding.

Luke was half asleep at first and I had to shake him. We whispered furiously for a while. But when he realised I'd already packed up our shared suitcase, taken it out into the hall and was not coming back into the apartment, he evidently decided that staying without me would be even worse for him in the morning than this cloak-and-dagger disappearance overnight.

Back down in the lift, back into the car – parked on a steep incline – where Luke sat at the wheel for a minute with his eyes closed as if summoning strength, then to the only hotel I could, in that moment, think of, the big yellow Holiday Inn.

I locked the chain on our bedroom door. The bed was hard and low. Flyers for a 24-hour casino called NEW ERA and various strip clubs were fanned across the coffee table. Maybe it was the sight of these that made me think of tugging at Luke's waistband – to make it up to him, or to separate in his mind who I was now from the child I turned into with my family.

Immediately afterward he fell asleep and I got up and stood for a long time at the window.

As a child I would stay up watching the fires. Silhouettes of buildings, indistinguishable from the night except where they glowed. Their black geometry slowly folding. In the morning familiar places would look foreign, as if I'd never seen them.

*

I woke to three powder shafts of sunlight on my cheek. A line of moth holes in the heavy curtain shone white-hot like bullet holes. Leaving Luke to sleep I left the bed and tweezed two hairs from my jaw, crouching in front of the mirror.

The lights in the windowless bathroom went out midway through my shower and the hot water ran cold. In the pitch-dark I groped my way, dripping, to unlock the door.

Downstairs, the receptionist explained that the whole area had the same problem. Maybe workmen had cut through something – they were excavating under the roads all round the hotel. They had a generator but it was not, at this present time, working. One American woman who came to the desk behind me was outraged that she could not take the elevator up to her room. Was she supposed to walk up nine floors? My home had been on the tenth, I wanted to tell her.

Luke gave me the silent treatment all the way to the airport. When I asked what was wrong he said: Nothing, but there will be if you keep asking me, so I stopped asking.

Our Austrian Airlines flight from Sarajevo Airport stopped in Vienna for an hour. Luke was miles ahead of me and I went through what turned out to be the wrong exit – for passport check not connecting flights. Luke had my boarding pass, so I had to go all the way through security again and back to the gate where he seemed to be in an even worse mood, headphones clamped over his ears.

Boarding again for the final leg, dusk shimmered over the runway and I remembered that first evening in Sanary. With a sharp intake of breath as if I was being submerged in ice, I realised I'd left the ring with Hana.

I couldn't bring myself to tell him what I'd done this time. It made me feel like my mother.

The cabin filled with the strains of Mozart. Conveniently, since we were ignoring each other, Luke was seated several rows ahead. I guess because he hadn't known how much time he could take off so soon after our summer holiday, he'd booked his own return some time after he'd done mine. That was the reason – but I kept looking up and between the seats to where I could see the curve of his ear, waiting for him to turn.

Poised on the runway, I looked over the tarmac. At the green lights glittering their messages across it in the darkness.

After we collected the bags, and the train pulled into Liverpool Street, he finally took my hand.

The chokehold loosened. My words came out in a rush. I asked him again if he still loved me. Again he took his time to respond.

There was a lot of tension, he said finally. And I'm not used to that.

ASYLUM ROAD

10

It felt like returning to reality. London, but without a diamond flashing in my peripheral vision all the time.

Luke went straight to his office while I went with the bag to the flat. Entering, closing the door behind me, everything slipped back into place. I knew then I would never go back.

Luxuries I'd stopped noticing now seemed lit from within. The pressure in the shower seemed stronger. I stood under its cascade until I forgot where I was. The bathroom blurred and my breathing became shallow. I stopped the water and pressed my face into a heavy towel, its detergent smell, until I felt strong enough to tackle the blocked sink.

The various things I'd puked up had become one thick, primordial tar, but as the putrid remains began to glug away, I felt energised. A certainty came over me that order had been restored.

I couldn't bring myself to think about the ring yet. Instead I opened my laptop, emailed the lost property counter at Split. When the reply came that still nothing had been found, the feeling I'd had of something being stuck in my airways every time I remembered the lost items now dissipated.

That my confused thinking might ever amount to *a significant original contribution to knowledge* had seemed implausible from the start. It now struck me as ridiculous that I would have to have these same unoriginal thoughts all over again. To eke out the same niche and then defend it felt like the most futile thing I could imagine. Reproducing all those lost words (concomitant, coterminous, coeval) that no one would ever read and which could serve no real purpose to anyone.

University institutions had provided me with shelter and a certain amount of liberty, a veneer of cosmopolitanism, but I had not made many friends. By then I only spent time with Christopher, and sometimes his friends, or Luke and his. The two groups could not have been more different and they never mixed. I called the latter posh but Luke insisted they were middle class. Anyway, the correct word for truly posh people was *grand*, he said, and actually grand people were often broke.

Initially these posh friends of his acted interested in getting to know me. They made me feel welcome, if not at home. But five years on they rarely asked more than polite questions. How was your summer? How's the PhD? I realised they had only been starting conversations with me as a reflex of confidence, according to a code of behaviour they all knew. It didn't mean they were truly interested, just that they could speak to strangers with ease. In such an incestuous group they might pounce on one as a novelty – a *random* or a *fringe person* as they were known – but I was no longer new.

I'd made temporary alliances with some of them. New girlfriends mainly. This was how I'd made most of my friends – uniting with outsiders via a shared sense of exclusion. It could feel heady at first but that quickly turned to bitterness if they managed to assimilate.

I sent two emails with the same two words as the subject, ignoring the two warnings: *this body has no text*.

QUITTING PHD

I waited for two responses.

But you're so close, Luke protested. *It'd be perverse*.

Minutes later Christopher's:

Sunk cost fallacy. Where the fuck have you been? How was BiH?

I replied to Christopher's, explaining about my phone, the lost book, the desire to be free of it, and Luke's insistence I carry on. He said Luke's reservation would probably be that he thought I was looking to become even more dependent. You should tell him you'll get a job, he wrote. A full-time one, not more transcribing.

I tried to think of what else I could pretend to do while Luke went out to work.

Usually when he left the house I would listen for a few moments, imagining I might hear his key turn in the lock, footsteps bounding back up the stairs. Then I'd gaze at my phone's darkness, waiting for communication from someone. Once I was sure Luke was not coming back, I went round neutralising the absence. Closing things he'd left open or turning things off he'd left on. Replacing lids. Hanging up the wet towel, lowering the seat, picking up waste material.

The routine continued: check face, check chin, pluck renegade hairs – digging when they weren't ready, wiping blood from the blade. Brush teeth, wash hair, make tea, sift mail. Another flyer warning us we lived in a hard water area. Sort laundry, fill French press, find something broken, add to list, panic as the washing machine reached its frenzy.

If I didn't have a wash to do, the silence could grow deafening, waiting for him to make contact. Until he did, it felt as if I was very far from life and the outside world. If he didn't, my refuge could become imprisonment. To escape I'd close my eyes and see if I could imagine the future. Perhaps that's what my mother meant when she said the women in our family had foresight. Two more thoughts usually occurred to me then.

1. No one can give me what I need.
2. I need to need less.

I made quieter, smaller movements. Tried to take up less space. I once listened to an eight-hour YouTube video called Ambient Iso Binaural Beats and watched the sky pass beyond the window, imagining myself no longer *encircled by negative thoughts*. Still the unrelenting sensitivity as if my skin had peeled right off.

It was better if I wasn't already in the flat when he came back to it. Like a good exile, I began spending all my time in cafes. I felt better too this way, returning to the flat on a more equal footing. Like a dog that had taken itself for a walk.

Christopher called it limerence, the magical beginning I wanted back. When each hair I found after he used the shower, usually coiled in the grout between tiles, I gathered like relics of a saint. When I talked about him as *my boyfriend* and my heart had raced.

Luke had insisted we call his flat *ours*. In practice, both of us tended toward the evasive but definite article *the*. He had teased me, in the beginning, over how I couldn't bring myself to actually use things I owned, preferring to keep them for a future date. I used so little toothpaste, he said, it was unlikely my teeth were ever clean. I watched the smart meter he'd installed which told me how much energy I consumed each day I was alone there. It would go up dramatically in the morning if I had a shower or boiled an egg, and I would think that it was pointless to eat eggs. The benefit was essentially cancelled out by the energy and expense of cooking them. I started to buy food that could be eaten raw.

Still, it was hard to express my happiness then. There was no room. I remember it like floating in warm water. A weightless, all-over miracle, my body held by something that also ran through my fingers. I liked hearing the sounds he made getting ready for work. The shower turning on then its softening which told me his body was beneath it. The electric shaver, the kettle, cup down, the steam hiss of the iron. All meant progress underway, without me having to make any. I rarely had anywhere to be at that hour. And then, exactly twelve hours later, I'd assume positions suggestive of domestic bliss for the moment his key turned in the lock. Not bent over my notebook on the sofa but hanging washing, arranging a salad, or emerging from a bath to print my body against his shirt. Inhaling the smell of exertion, his fug of productivity.

Somehow I had imagined this state would be made permanent by the decision to get married.

Luke arrived back just before midnight. I was in bed, not wishing to give the impression I'd been waiting. Over the course of the day my optimism had begun to falter. I'd started to feel uneasy again. I'd gone for several walks, trying to rid myself of a burning sensation. Not hot but cold, deep in my chest, like smoking a menthol cigarette. Shrinking, twisting blue, crushing in on itself. It grew painful as I heard him unlock the door in the hall and climb the stairs. I'd draped a drying sheet over the banister – a white flag of surrender.

When he came in he sat on the bed, began to untie his laces without greeting. I waited as long as I could bear the silence.

Are you OK?

A longer silence. I began to vibrate in the dark. He got into bed and sat with his back against the wall.

Luke?

I'm trying to relax.

OK.

A longer silence still, in which I turned to face the other way, then turned to face him again, the coldness spreading out now from my chest into my veins.

Luke?

These pregnant silences drove me mad at first and then I tended to panic as if I was being strangled.

I don't know what to say, he said at last, staring at the wall.

I realised I was panting and tried to take smaller breaths than I felt I needed.

It's not working, he said then, in an unfamiliar voice.

What isn't?

I tried to swallow but my tongue felt swollen, blocking up my throat. By now my whole body shook, as if something inside – a whole other person – threatened to break out of it.

Well, I said brightly, aren't we going to talk about this?

I was determined not to behave in a way that was hysterical or backed him into a corner. That, as Luke had taught me, is when even docile animals lash out. It was better to sit with the uncertainty than provoke a reaction I didn't want.

It's late, he said with a shrug of resignation. Talk tomorrow. I need to sleep.

Yes, I said, as if this had been what I'd suggested, better to talk about things in daylight.

I lay awake all night again, listening to him sleep, but must've dozed sometime after five because I woke up to find him gone. Immediately the adrenaline returned. Then I heard him on the landing.

Where are you going? It's Saturday.

Work.

The word landed on me in the empty bed like something insignificant dropped from a height. Then a zip closed decisively and he returned, giving me a conciliatory pat. I said nothing, moved my chin a centimetre, offering him my mouth.

I haven't brushed my teeth.

I persisted and he submitted to the kiss, which made it worse.

You can't work here?

I left my charger at the office.

OK, well then, I'll see you later?

Maybe you should stay at Christopher's tonight.

OK . . . that's a good idea . . . right then, I'll do that.

He picked up his running headphones. I hid my face in the pillow, arm at a strange angle, unable to breathe until the front door had shut behind him.

I spent the whole day with the sensation that the floor beneath me was giving way. Nothing I came into contact with felt solid. Nothing could hold me. From the bedroom window I saw that a neighbour's roof had been removed and was now covered with plastic sheeting that moved like a lung in the wind. I watched it for a while, breathing in and out in sync. As one magpie sailed past the window I shut my eyes. When I opened them I saw it had been joined by what I assumed was its mate and felt this to be a good omen. Then I saw it was in fact cannibalising a pigeon and I reached out and struck the window.

Luke emailed in the afternoon just as the light was fading.

I think it's best if you stay at Christopher's for a couple of days.

I lay on the carpet until its weave was printed on my skin, trying to get rid of the falling feeling, interrogating the phrase he'd used. Couple of days. Couple. I often used that word interchangeably with *few* and *several*. Did Luke's couple strictly mean just two?

I could not think of any responses so I didn't send one. I'd communicate with potent silence the way he always did, saying only what was absolutely necessary and factual.

I emailed Christopher instead who said he would order an Uber for me. Twenty minutes later I got in with a bag – mostly the same things I'd taken to my parents'. The luggage tag from Split still attached. I kept my eyes out the window but the driver seemed anxious to make conversation, presumably not because he had much interest in his passenger but so he would get a good rating. He tried to catch my eye in the mirror. A cherry air freshener swayed beneath it.

Going on holiday? he said.

Yes.

The shop window below Christopher's place was daubed with the words FINAL DAYS.

It's a break, I said after he'd held my body for a long time, very tightly.

He'd taken the afternoon off work to sit in this alternate reality beside me. I wanted to express gratitude but could barely speak. I let myself be brought onto the sofa.

Do you want to take your coat off?

No.

Can I get you tea? Alcohol?

I shook my head.

I have a work phone you can borrow while you're here, he said, if you need.

I nodded, trying not to let his kindness undo me, and he nodded too, and then we watched nature documentaries. He didn't even comment on how relentlessly I traced my nail along my jaw.

Do you need anything? he asked when the third episode began automatically, I'm making dal.

I shook my head.

Would you rather listen to a podcast? What's that one you're –

I shook my head again, more firmly.

I woke up in the morning to find the sofa under me was moving. The place next door was a building site, I remembered. Someone must be tugging at the foundations.

Luke suggested we meet three days later, during his lunch hour, near his work. I told Christopher he had suggested a walk. I sensed his mother behind this idea, assuming being in public might stop a scene from taking place. Or so her son could not be trapped by me then held hostage.

On my way I passed a headline printed on a board: EXPERTS WARN AGAINST OPTIMISM.

His office was down a side street near the Heron Tower, shared with a few other green-investment-type companies. I was early, so I waited outside that building, rather than loiter directly outside his. The lobby was taken up by a vast aquarium which I knew Luke hated.

He knew I had no phone so I assumed he would not be late. At the appointed time, I stood waiting in the street.

He came out unhurriedly at last, wearing his suit. Looking more like a stranger than he usually did. It was more pronounced, maybe, in this world where I did not belong.

He directed us eastward and bought vegetarian gyoza for us both from a street food market. My stomach was tight as a ball.

He led me into a small park inside a square I'd never seen before. I remember the light gliding through the mulberry trees, down to where their bellies crept along the ground.

I watched as he tried his first real sentence. This took a long time. I formed what was supposed to be an expression of encouragement. A lack of reproach. Inside, the cold fire burned my chest.

At last I prompted him, *so is this over?* and he just sat there in silence again, before finally saying *I guess* – despondently, as if it was all my idea.

I sat for several moments, looking into the distance. Then, before I could stop myself, blurted out *is there someone else?* and he looked angry, as if I should know the answer to such a vulgar question, when I had no idea, any longer, what I knew.

What did he say?

That he has some stuff to work out.

He wants you to give him space?

Yes. That's all it is. I think he needs space to think.

In response Christopher emailed a link to a story about a lovesick Chinese woman who'd spent a week in KFC because she needed time to think.

Christopher invented the game What Can Anya Eat? The answer was usually one small plate of cucumber, thinly shaved.

He brought things to me for the first few days, then insisted I come to the kitchen, like a stray he was patiently rehoming. The game was satisfying, he said. It was satisfying for me too, to feel myself wasting away.

When he insisted I accompany him to the supermarket to guide him, everything on the shelves seemed useless, as if it was only packaging. I could not imagine what purpose any of it served.

Most nights I lay awake on the sofa reading old emails, comparing them to happier ones, putting words into the search box, as if this was a problem I could solve with research. When I did sleep, I felt as if I was still aware of everything, like the dolphins from the documentary Christopher and I had watched. They slept one brain hemisphere at a time, allowing them to swim continuously. I didn't dream, I just lay there in wait until the birds started up, as if nothing was out of the ordinary. When I woke, before I even remembered, there was already something pinning me down, a weight on my chest. It felt like waking inside a corpse. If I started awake in the middle of the night, I would imagine I was next to him as he whimpered. His shoulder would shine in the darkness and I'd say soothing things, tell him where he was. Wait for him to understand. Sometimes I groped for him in the empty space. My second thought on waking was that the day would end the same.

After several weeks I wanted to move. Not far from the sofa but in small circles around the room – joints swollen, head too light on my neck. My arms felt weightless, as if I'd just put down two heavy bags. This lightness sickened me, but I also felt disgusted by the more substantial parts, the way my thighs touched as I walked.

Soon I ventured up and down the street and to the nearest park. I felt myself to be allergic to strange bodies which were, and then were not, him.

I watched a skein of geese pass over me. There was, the formation seemed to say, safety in numbers, safer than within a single pair.

I thought of him out with his friends while I took my lonely weekend walks. Imagining the complaints he would have made about me, the assembled men revolted by my flagrant needs.

Out of nowhere, I began to run. No one was chasing me, I just felt myself speed up. It gave me a brief feeling of control, of self-direction.

December came with no word from him. Though I barely left the house except to exercise, I'd inched closer to the borrowing limit on my credit card. Christopher tried to make me come to *gatherings*, which I knew really meant drug-fuelled parties with hundreds of people. I said I couldn't bear the idea of strangers, when I really meant the smell. There were new proportions to smell now, I noticed. Sometimes I caught a sweet smell of rot when I was alone in my makeshift room, its origin unclear.

How much sooner I might've realised if I hadn't been used to near-permanent nausea.

At first, when it had been too long since my last period, I put the absence down to the Dubrovnik Escapelle. To the upheaval. The shock. Over-exercise. Near starvation. Then one afternoon I gave in and bought a pregnancy test.

As I waited on Christopher's bathroom floor, I studied myself in the mirror for the first time in weeks. I had muscles everywhere. Hollow cheeks. Rough, red patches on my palms. More blue veins in my wrists. The test turned positive. I stood rooted, the slight weight of it in my hand, wishing that every time I'd had a fearful instinct to confirm, I could have peed on a stick.

Until I'd quit, the plan had always been to finish the PhD before considering a family, except at certain points when I'd thought it would be easier to have a child. Luke was ambivalent too, for environmental reasons, but also knew how that would go down with Anne.

Now I found I did not want to evict the seed-sized thing, and nor did I want it to grow much more. What I wanted, if I wanted anything then, was to stay in pregnant limbo for as long as possible. To be pregnant was to be shielded by other, non-pregnant people.

I didn't tell anyone. Even Christopher. Every day I opened the cap to check the fibrous pink of the test until its validation faded. When it did, it felt like harbouring a criminal, both intimate and alien.

I had the sense that when I moved I glided. My breasts became two live creatures. They prickled against shirts.

My sister emailed about the ring Hana had finally turned in but I could not bring myself to answer. Something about the email, however, or just what it reminded me of, decided the question of the pregnancy.

The hold-music on the phone was relaxing at first. But after ten minutes it transitioned to electric guitar. By contrast the waiting room, when I arrived at the clinic, was very quiet. The sonographer moved along my abdomen, frowning at a monitor I could not see. I watched her face instead, deciphering the mystery of my insides in aseptic black and white. I imagined my womb like a dark basement.

Your bladder is full, she said.

The first time I'd been present for something like this had been in Glasgow. My aunt had given her teenage son a pet chameleon for his birthday. We were disappointed that his colouring never seemed to change. In the light, he did get a bit brighter maybe. Nikolaj, who was not yet Calum then, had christened him AJ. Who knows why. It made me think of AJ from the Backstreet Boys, and there was a similarity. But after only a few months, AJ grew gravely ill. He sat in a corner of his cage and wouldn't eat anything he was offered. My aunt put us all in the car and took him to the vet, who took an X-ray and announced that AJ was full of rocks. Why's he eating rocks? we asked. My aunt said she didn't know. She had to syringe feed him, and at first he seemed stronger, but then he stopped swallowing that too.

My aunt got a second opinion. The second vet said AJ had stopped eating as her belly was full of eggs. He, my cousin said, correcting her. No, she. AJ was a female chameleon, she repeated. This was a shock, and then we tried to understand how she'd managed to get pregnant too. The vet grew more stern with us, irritated by our ignorance. She's not laying the eggs because she hasn't got a laying tray. Female lizards need a tray. She pointed at the scan, her pen circling where the mature follicles clustered like grapes.

Discovering his pet was in fact a girl, Nikolaj immediately lost interest.

In the wild she'd have dug a deep hole, the vet continued, but she can't do that in captivity. Or not in this cage. She's holding them in until she can nest.

AJ died that afternoon. I helped bury her under the hibiscus.

On my way back to Christopher's, I took out my credit card and bought heat pads, eye pads, sanitary pads, notepads. White socks, white shirts, not, in the end, white underwear. Seeing some of this spread out on the floor when he came home, Christopher stopped and surveyed the scene, but he did not say anything except to enquire what oligarch's child I was now tutoring.

For my last trip to the clinic I wore a supersized pad in preparedness. The new doctor spoke very fast, almost slurring while explaining the various elements of the procedure in so much detail that she must have found the repetition monotonous and I found her incomprehensible.

I lodged the first tablet against my gums, which made it hard to ask questions anyway. The nurse insisted that if no one was collecting me, I had to get a taxi, could I give her my home address? Initially I gave the wrong one out of habit.

The roads were blocked with traffic. I began to feel hot, then faint. I thought again of the chameleon. My ears started ringing. Loudly. Suddenly I needed a bathroom. I have to get out, I said. I have to get out of the car. I stumbled the last few streets, tried to open the front door. I can't see, I said, now to nobody, and spat the remainder out.

Somehow I got the door open, ears still ringing, mouth foaming, and then there were rooms of pain. My vision swam. In and out, black spots, intense heat and then a chill, and then a kind of equilibrium where the pain subsided, before the fire returned, hotter than before. I felt it rising, moving up my body. Catching, rising upward, smoke. In my ears now, something hissing.

I woke and Christopher was there. I don't know how I ended up on the sofa, lowing like a cow. The jumbo pad crackled when I moved.

Do you want anything?

I shook my head.

Did Luke contact you?

Yes.

He looked at me for a beat, unsure if I was telling him the truth.

I woke up in the dark and knew immediately that I'd bled through. Returning to the sofa from the bathroom, I unzipped the soiled coverings from the cushions and reached for my laptop, then felt my stomach lurch. An email from him. Blank, but forwarding one from Mira, addressed to us both, apologising since she only had Luke's address. I read her words over several times, wondering how Luke would have experienced reading it.

She no longer felt secure or like she could achieve what she wanted work-wise, while living in Belgrade. She'd thought about moving to the Czech offices but that probably wasn't far enough. She was considering Berlin where she knew one or two people, and London, where she knew us and some publishing friends. It occurred to me Mira would've used the threats as her excuse for leaving to her mother. She would be in London before Christmas, at least until January to have meetings, scope things out, hopefully find a place to live, might she stay with us? If not, no problem, she could sort something else. She signed off with love and hoped our wedding plans were shaping up.

I knew Luke would not respond, but I kept putting off a reply. Then a few days later, Christopher said one of his commune friends was looking to sublet. Cheap, in your price range, he added. They were looking for someone long-term, in case, he softened his voice, that ended up being my situation.

Christopher stayed with his mother in Manchester for two weeks over Christmas every year. I was welcome to remain on his sofa, but what did I think about the room?

It was true I had a deep pain in my lower back, near-constant behind my kidney, from sleeping on a sofa bed which had lost a wheel so that, unfolded, it tilted toward the floor. But the idea of moving into a commune, however temporarily, during the time I was most tempted to become a hermit, was unbearable.

When I finally replied to Mira and explained the situation, I'd meant to put her off. Instead she said she would love to share the sublet, what a perfect solution that was. She'd arrived a few days ago and was staying in an Airbnb on a noisy street, having no luck on SpareRoom. Presumably my friend wanted their sofa back and she'd take the flat long-term.

I arranged to meet her in a restaurant I'd found near where she was staying in Shepherd's Bush. It was too far to walk and too cold. On the bus heading west, I sat on the top deck. I still felt nauseous, still had a too-keen sense of smell, but now I felt my body humming with concentration. There was a clap of thunder and the glass became wet with rain. A woman seated alone a few seats ahead threw back her head and crowed:

Pussy HOLE!

Then again, more insistently.

PU-SSY-HO-OO-LE!

The last hole had infinite vowels in it, like the blast of an ocean liner.

Normally this woman would have unnerved me, but just then I found I admired her.

When Mira arrived, I could tell she was disappointed.

Is this a chain? she asked over my Serbian greeting, I'm only speaking English now.

We left.

I don't really want to talk about it, I said as we resettled ourselves at a bar of her choosing. I'm trying to put it out of my mind. This felt as close as I could get to the kind of assertiveness that she had.

She opened her bag and handed me an uncorrected proof. I recognised the name.

Not light reading, she warned, but should be a distraction.

She told me the last time she was in London was five years ago, during the Olympics. It felt very different now, like the scales had fallen from most people's eyes.

How was it with your family?

Oh, I grimaced. A waste of carbon as far as Luke's concerned.

I meant how was it for you with them? Would Daria leave Sarajevo now?

I don't think so. No.

There's a whole Serbian crew that moved to Peckham, did I tell you? They squatted there. I met some of them in Belgrade. I told one guy the name of the road and he knew the place we're moving to.

I said nothing.

I think this will be good for you Anja. Independence.

But I'll be living with you.

I mean living for yourself – not pleasing other people.

It occurred to me I wanted Luke to hear I'd moved out of Christopher's. I didn't like that he could picture where I was while I had so many blanks for his activity.

The waiter arrived, his bald head glossy under a low-hanging bulb. I let Mira order. When he left again, she took out her phone, pulled up her photos and passed them to me. She'd been to see the commune that morning.

But that word . . . she rolled her eyes. A 'commune' is a stretch.

Listening to her as I scrolled through the photos I felt a surge of possibility. I noted the ease with which I could speak, or not speak, and have her instinctively understand my mood.

To us, she said, raising her glass. I still can't believe the road.

I'd let myself be copied into emails without reading them, choosing from the automated menu for suggested response.

What about it?

Asylum Road? By the way, you've lost too much weight.

I looked down again at my plate and pushed some chickpeas around it.

Anyway, next thing to sort out is getting your stuff back.

I nodded meekly.

She helped me compose a message to Luke that she would send, editing down everything I'd written to:

I'll be coming tomorrow for Anja's things.

Then she paid the bill for food only she had eaten.

Are you sure you don't want to come with me tonight?

She was going to a party with someone she'd met on a dating app that week.

I kept my mouth shut, feeling a tremor in my lip.

Well OK, I'll meet you at Luke's and we'll get a taxi from there together tomorrow. Yes?

I nodded again, unable to say thanks.

When I got back, Christopher was still at work and I started watching another documentary. So far I'd avoided ones with human beings as their subject, finding animals much safer, but this time I felt brave enough to try something about a once-famous folk singer. It turned out she lost her voice after her husband left her. I turned it off, reached for Mira's book and lay with it unopened.

Then a response from Luke arrived, forwarded by Mira.

Fine with me, let me know if I can help.

His efficiency was merciless. Google suggested three responses:

OK

Bye

Thanks!

When Christopher returned he sat on the end of the sofa and told me about a case that was going on. The defendant was representing himself and identified only as a freeman of the land. Freemen, Christopher was coming to learn, believed that laws only bind people because the state had issued them with a birth certificate. By this logic, if they rejected a state-given name, they would become free of the law.

How was your friend?

We're taking it.

The commune?

Yes.

Anya the anarchist!

I'm never going to be able to repay you, I hope you're aware of that.

Fuck off, he grinned. It's been nice to have you here. When you go I'll have to get a cat.

I woke up at four in the morning with a knife twisting in my side. It was hard to breathe and I worried the abortion had caused *internal rupturing*. I got up, put Christopher's parka over my pyjamas, and walked out into the night. Without knowing where I was going, I carried on for several hours and reached the Albert Embankment. The majority of tourists don't seem to know that those benches, on little individual plinths, give the best view of the Houses of Parliament. I was careful to stand in a non-suicidal pose, though there were few pedestrians in sight. Luke once told me the eels in the Thames were full of hormones and cocaine. I resisted the mental image but now I saw a roiling orgy of eels beneath the surface. Still, the walking had soothed my stomach, or the cold had numbed it, and for the first time since leaving Luke's, I understood that I was free now to do whatever I wanted. I wanted to be here, exactly where I stood, watching grey water moving somewhere.

11

A child's glove hung on the railings.

You're sure he's not going to be in? Mira said cautiously behind me as I stopped at the gate before the tiled path to Luke's front door. Painted the tasteful grey I'd selected before it became so prevalent in that neighbourhood, the typographic number in frosted glass above.

She was carrying several of those large, tartan-patterned plastic bags. The kind my mother had with the fraying plastic threads.

She looked at me, eyebrows raised, as if there might be an ambush waiting.

I doubt he'd do that.

Well, you know him best.

I wondered if I could really say that.

We climbed the steps and I fumbled with the keys, my fingers numb and inflexible, forgetting, for a minute, which way the lock turned.

On the mat there were notes from numerous parcel delivery companies. *We missed you. We missed you.* I'd always signed for his deliveries.

Luke had lined up some of my things in the hall. I walked past them into the living room. It was the sameness of everything that depressed me, as if my absence had left no mark.

It was only two in the afternoon but the winter sunlight was thin and Mira pressed down all the light switches but somehow that made it darker. Across the street I could see my former neighbour standing at his open window, watching us as if he thought we were intruders.

I looked at what Luke had left out. Mainly things from the attic and under the bed, in case I forgot them I guessed. There was something so final about this – so deliberate and determined that this was no longer my home to come back to, that I broke down for a moment. Mira squeezed my shoulder and I collected myself, noticing the roll of black bin liners in her other arm.

You look like you've come to rig the place, I said, wiping away tears.

Did you just make a joke? That's good. Tell me what you want to take and we'll get it over with.

I realised she'd switched out of English. We were back to our private language, which helped somehow in this familiar place I was now estranged from.

Who owns the plants?

He does, but I watered them.

So they come with you now. Same for everything else you took care of.

A defiant energy coursed through my body as it had the night before on the bus when the passenger ahead had screamed. Now he'd seceded, withdrawing protection, I didn't have to treat him or anything that belonged to him with reverence. I felt a flicker of temptation to break something. I wanted to do something rebellious, mainly to show him I was capable of doing it. As I took my pictures off the walls, I saw the nails I'd driven into the plaster and the black marks left by the frames. I scanned the rooms, the insides of drawers, picked up items at random. A lip balm bought in Copenhagen – a holiday tacked on to a conference he was speaking at. My noise-cancelling headphones – which I'd selflessly put over his ears to drown out the neighbours' parties. I put them down or resisted touching them altogether. Each banal object was a noose on the ground, ready to sweep me upside down with it.

Then I went into the bedroom. I stared at the crease marks like a sandbank in the centre of the bed. I tried to decide whether it looked like more than one body had been sleeping there.

I think the bed sheets haven't been changed since I left, I shouted.

Gross, she yelled back, then came upstairs to join me.

Changing your sheets alone is a struggle, she said dryly. You're lucky we'll be sharing a bed from now on. It made me feel so lonely the first time, and the weight of everything, all the thoughts I'd been holding off, suddenly dropped down all at once. I fell backward onto the bed in fact, with my arms and head inside the cover. Then I cried – the first time in a long, long time. I felt panicked, and sort of thrashed around trying to get out, and then I just surrendered. I must have fallen asleep. I think that's when the self-narration started, I had to talk myself out of there.

She asked if she could have a Fanta from the fridge. There were loads.

I'd never known him to buy Fanta and for a moment I lost my balance.

Sure, I said.

She went back to the kitchen.

I opened his bedside drawer. Looking for something incriminating I suppose, but the only thing I didn't recognise was a small blue book which I took and brought down slowly toward Mira.

I just found it in the drawer.

She took the Bible and turned it over, then opened it. Carefully, as if it might contain drugs.

I opened it already.

And this is a new thing? That you know of.

I nodded dumbly and sat at the table, digging into the base of my skull.

Well, she shrugged. That might explain some things.

I imagine it's his mum's. They're both quite into eschatology.

Do they know you're on a break?

I don't know what they know, they haven't been in touch.

It started to rain, a real rainstorm, drumming on the windows and darkening the cardboard boxes we'd already put outside.

She rolled her eyes and went to shield the boxes. Thunder and lightning in quick succession.

Whenever Mira stood beside me, I felt as if I might be better off in some essential way from now on. The minute she stepped out, this calm evaporated.

I wondered where to leave my keys. The kitchen table seemed too much like a message. I put them casually at one end of the sofa, then took them back again. I might still need them, I reasoned.

After everything had been gathered and stacked by the door, she ordered a six-seater taxi which appeared almost immediately so there was no time for any ritual.

She sat in the passenger seat and I sat in the only back seat not folded down, surrounded by belongings. As she confirmed the address with the driver, he turned and pulled a face. Asylum not as in lunatic, she explained, but almshouses before the welfare state. He laughed and said where we were going was no good.

Peckham is only bad people. Bad place, full of bad people. Always fighting each other. Like civil war.

Where do you live? Mira asked him.

Enfield. But I'm from Iraq.

I was not taking part in the conversation and did not want it to continue in this vein, but Mira was suddenly interested.

Did you move here during the war then?

He shook his head. After. I was an interpreter, for your country.

Oh, she smiled, we're not from here.

He was silent and I hoped he would not ask the obvious.

So, Mira persisted when he did not, they gave you asylum then?

He nodded, staring at the traffic jam ahead. Sometimes I wish they did not.

Will you go back there at some point?

He glanced behind him in the mirror.

No.

Mira looked steadily at him.

They killed my family who stayed, he said quietly. It took me two years to get out with my wife and children.

There, I am a traitor. I thought the English would have gratitude, but I have no more use to them these days. It's me who is supposed to be grateful. My children want to go back. We get everything here – school, doctor, so on – but they imagine Iraq as paradise. They live here since they were very small, but miss home more than me. They have a – a very idealised . . . image of the place. My youngest wasn't even born there but she knows all the old songs. She taught them to herself.

We settled into uneasy silence as the car slotted into more traffic on the Old Kent Road. It was dark already. My energy had waned and I slumped against the armrest with my forehead on the glass. The glass was frozen and the sensation was unpleasant – like a drill boring into me – but still I kept it there.

The rain slowed. I took in the neon glare of shop windows, Nigerian churches and floodlit retail parks. Their light and colour in the beads of water on my window. As we turned off at the forecourt of a shuttered Toys R Us, Mira reached round and squeezed my hand.

I forgot to tell you, she said as we parked outside. They have a mouse. But it means they don't have rats. We aren't allowed to put down any traps or poison they told me. We're just supposed to let it be. It comes with the territory, kind of like a pet. Maybe another reason why it's cheap.

I nodded, thinking about the set-up from the perspective of the mouse. Imagining her alarm if, with our arrival, she found herself unwelcome, having considered herself an established member of the commune.

Luke had once discovered a mouse making a nest underneath the floorboards. Making a nest, he said, meant she was having babies. It was sad. She was putting herself in danger just by getting on with her life because now she needed to be dealt with.

The interpreter helped us make several trips back and forth across the road to the pavement below a tall, dark-bricked house. Mira held the iron gate open with one of my bin bags and we carried everything up the steps. The cold, after the warmth of the car, was awful. I waited, stamping my feet while Mira tried to unlock the door, noticing that the ground-floor window had been covered completely with cling film, so that it sparkled in the glow of the street lamp.

We piled my belongings in the hallway first, to get them out of the wet. I hoped no one would come out to greet us. As if she'd read my mind, Mira said everyone was out for the night.

They invited us, actually. Some opening. An exhibition. So we have the place to ourselves.

She could still sense my anxiety. Apart from her, the nurse, and Christopher, I'd hardly spoken with anyone in weeks.

It's not like that. Really, nothing too intimate. Each flat's on a separate floor with its own door. Trust me it's nothing you can't handle after the basement.

The lights in the hall were motion sensitive. When they went out, Mira nudged against the dark to activate them and I followed her up the stairs to the very top.

Shit, I said. I left the pictures by the gate.

I ran down again, almost falling where the carpet treads were loose. My new forgetfulness was becoming habit.

Gone already.

When I came back up, Mira was unpacking for me. Putting my books beside hers. I wandered past her to the one other room which was the bathroom, the only place in the flat which afforded privacy through a door with a patterned glass window. I went in and shut it.

It looks dirty but it's not, she called after me. I tried to clean the shower and nearly fumigated myself. It's the enamel, not dirt – it actually makes it worse trying to clean it because then more gets stripped away.

I stood over the basin, waiting for a familiar wave of nausea to pass. When it had I came back to the window which overlooked the garden, now too dark to see anything except what looked like a chicken coup on a patio directly below.

Hens, Mira said. What were the names of ours again?

Agata was mine. I can't remember what yours was called.

Her father had sold things on the black market to buy them, but it was too cold for them to lay eggs. And, he told us sadly, they were very stressed. Mira and I would try to soothe them, warming them between our thighs, stroking their heads. Singing. I think it calmed us more than them. When the shelling's over, Mira would tell them, we'll go to the beach. Lie in the sun, swim. We'll all relax together.

I remember carrying one of the rare eggs to my mother with great ceremony, but my hands were smooth and numb with cold and the egg slipped as I tried to turn the door handle. The horror of that moment, as if I'd dropped a whole planet.

I saw now that Mira had taken Luke's juicer and an expensive set of Japanese knives. She winked at me as she put them on the kitchen counter then ordered us Vietnamese and two beers.

What does your ex think about you moving here? I asked her.

Oh – she waved her hand dismissively. I don't care what he thinks. He'd say I'm overreacting. He criticises people who move away from the Balkans.

She checked her phone to see how far off the Deliveroo was.

Every time we fight it's like I cut another thread between us. I get more and more detached and so he feels it more and more – how I didn't, don't, care. He's just so angry. Before I left I gave him a stone from my collection – sodalite – to help him unwind. Obviously, it provoked him. He insisted on coming back to my flat. To help me finish packing, he said. He put the stone back and sat on the bed and told me how worried he was about me – mostly the men making threats but also my mental state. Then he was the one threatening me. He's just insecure that I don't need him for my protection. When I finally managed to get him to leave, do you know the last thing he said to me? He told me I should get my ears pinned!

She pulled back her dark hair and bent her, admittedly prominent, ears forward. I smiled, finding it difficult not to feel envious. He was still trying to make her feel something.

When the bell rang Mira went down to collect the food, but after she shut the door I could hear her talking still.

Did you say you wanted driving lessons? she said when she returned. What about with the Kurdish guy? It's his car in the drive. He's an instructor.

Can't afford it sadly.

I'd told her I'd been using those online tutorials to distract myself and Mira had agreed I needed to have a self-improvement project to see me through this period.

I don't think I'm up for it right now anyway – I waved my hand – having to make conversation.

She laughed. You're managing.

I'd hated the real lessons I'd had, long ago, and even the few I'd done with Luke in the quiet roads near his parents' house. I'd been confronted with the uselessness of my qualifications when it came to learning something practical. My mind would not cooperate.

Mira had already finished her food and was staring hungrily at my untouched plate. I pushed it toward her.

He's quite handsome actually, the Kurd. Seems quite straightforward too. I need a simple man I think, but I know they find me difficult. And if they don't they're already married and looking for something very complicated. I met one of those at that party the other night. Actually, that was a funny story. There was no bin in their fancy bathroom, which I only noticed *after* I'd taken out my tampon. I thought, OK you deserve to have your toilet blocked. I was angry because the guy who'd invited me – I matched with him on the Heathrow Express – turned out to be married after all. Then I saw all these toilet books in the guest bathroom. It's the only rule I want to impose while we're here. No reading in the toilet. Anyway I wrapped the tampon and went to bin it, but one of the catering staff saw me with a wad of tissue in my hand and told me to hand it over like it was a spat-out canapé. I *ran.* Oh, let me show you something.

She got up and went to a chest of drawers then came back with a Cuban cigar box with drawings and stickers decorating it.

Open it, she instructed.

Drago's shrapnel collection. I quickly put it down and shook my head, blinking.

Waking, I got the lurching feeling in my stomach of being in the wrong place. Mira, I remembered, not Luke, was in the next room taking a shower. The windowpanes were covered in condensation. The misty skyline beyond that, back to front, now seen from south of the river.

She reappeared in a yellow silk kimono.

Have a meeting. Soho, she announced, an electric toothbrush in her mouth.

Applying her make-up at the table she told me about the other inhabitants of *the asylum*. I had imagined them all to be of a type but she said they were an incongruous group, like those motley crews of dogs led along by professional walkers, all yoked together in a faintly comedic way.

There was the Kurd driving instructor who was also a classical violinist. He tried to practise in the day, he'd said, which made her worry he mainly did it at night. The very tall girl with pale pink hair was, she suspected, his girlfriend. She was studying at Goldsmiths. She was not Kurdish – her family were from Wales – but she talked non-stop about the YPJ.

I looked blank.

Don't worry, she'll tell you about it. That'll be her boyfriend now.

She gestured below to the sound of a violin.

We listened, and suddenly I remembered what I'd overheard in Cornwall, the open window that led me here.

But I was spared that train of thought as Mira shrieked and pointed down beside her chair. I looked down to see a mouse. I bent closer. Even though I was so close I could have touched it, the mouse seemed unconcerned.

That's not normal, Mira said. Why isn't it running away? Aren't they nocturnal?

I shrugged.

There's a parasite, I said, remembering something Luke had told me. It removes their fear of cats. Instead of running away from the smell of predators, infected ones are actually attracted to it.

We watched as the mouse began to move, stop-starting toward the door. Mira looked up *mice that lose their fear of cats*, read a while, and nodded.

Toxoplasma can sexually reproduce only in the cat gut, and for it to get there, the pathogen's rodent host must be eaten.

It affects humans too – are you serious?

I watched the mouse come back again, then disappear behind a skirting board.

Mira continued in a voice of mock-cheerfulness:

In humans, studies have linked Toxoplasma infection with behavioural changes, risk-taking and schizophrenia. One study found an increased risk of traffic accidents in people infected with the parasite, another found changes in responses to cat odour.

She rolled her eyes. That's why we aren't allowed to kill it. It trusts that we're not going to.

After she left, I dressed in random items pulled from bags, found my trainers and ran downstairs. I didn't want to meet anyone.

The temperature had dropped again. First, I ran the length of the road back the way we'd driven the previous evening, turning around at a church inside a commercial property called THE MOUNTAIN OF PERFECTION. I peered through the iron railings outside the almshouses. In the middle there was a chapel, surrounded by a lawn and low buildings. One side of the entrance I could see had been left open.

Inside, it looked like the building had been gutted by fire. Bombed during the blitz, as the noticeboard told me, it was now a wedding venue. Everything had been destroyed internally (except a few stone monuments) but not one of the stained-glass windows had shattered. I felt even colder inside, and desolate, as if I'd entered the depths of an aquarium.

I turned right then left, running until I reached the butchers and beauty salons of Peckham Rye, only stopping when I reached the park, then walking a bit further as my heart rate settled. The sun broke out from behind the clouds and I sat down on a bench. As I sat there, feeling newly calm, my breath rising up in clouds, another person joined me, and just as his presence and the silence was starting to make me feel I should continue, he turned his face to mine.

Hey, he blurted, almost aggressive. What's your story?

He was American, I couldn't tell where from exactly, but he sounded like he'd been practising with a pick-up artist. I tried to convey that I was not in the mood for talking, smiling then taking from my bag the book Mira had given me.

What's your book then?

I showed him the cover. He looked at the title, in Serbian, and appeared to ponder it. I held my breath.

You like reading?

I shrugged, keeping my eyes on the page.

What's it about?

Genocide.

OK. Any good?

Depends what you're into I guess.

Does it have a good plot?

It's non-fiction.

He laughed as if he'd finally got the measure of me. What's your name, if you don't mind?

I made a face like I did, but he continued looking at me with his light eyes.

Anya.

His eyes reminded me of my dentist's as they bore down on me from above the surgical mask. Whenever he had me in the chair and had begun to suffocate me by placing some kind of clay in my mouth, or probing me with his latex fingers while I lay choking on my spit, he would start asking me personal questions like *so when are you getting married?*

I reopened the book determinedly, deciding this was the right time to put my new, Mira-inspired personality into action. I had to save myself. My neighbour was not deterred, stroking his cheek as if to indicate that he was still turning my name over.

Well listen Anya, I actually came over to talk to you for a reason. You look a little lost, if I may say. He was getting smoother, more relaxed with me. Evidently he thought his strategy was succeeding.

I shrugged again.

Are you from here?

I hesitated. No. Not here exactly.

Where's home?

I could not yet bring myself to walk away.

Where are *you* from? I said, turning the question.

Nashville. He smiled like I was finally playing along. Now you.

Glasgow.

OK and where's that?

About as far as you can get from Nashville, spiritually.

Well, Anya, it's funny you should mention that –

I clenched my jaw. He was not a pick-up artist then, but a stealth-mode Jehovah's Witness. He reached into his jacket pocket and passed me a piece of paper.

GAME CHANGER, I read.

I'm just starting out as a life coach. And if you go to my website you will see I'm also a gardener. Do you know what life coaching involves?

I tipped my head to one side, not sure which answer would be rewarded with the shorter conversation.

The stories we tell ourselves, he continued, in a monotone as if reading from a script, are what make us who we are. They tend to become a self-fulfilling prophecy.

I gave him my old number so that I could leave, then forced myself into a phone shop where I got out my credit card again, bought the cheapest they had, and had at least some of my life restored to me.

It got dark quickly. With my new phone in a shopping bag, I found myself at the BMX track in Burgess Park. The helmets shone in the floodlights, swooping over the pale hills like starlings in formation. I stood observing them, alone. The lights made the sky feel very close. I sat down again on a bench under their brightness, took the phone out of its packaging and stared at it before doubling over and throwing up onto the frozen ground.

12

I bought another pregnancy test. The cheapest one that came as a single rather than a pair. The woman at the clinic had advised doing one again four weeks later and that, even if it was negative, I still had to be vigilant in case I needed an ERPC. When I asked what that was she told me it stood for Evacuation of Retained Products of Conception.

I swallowed several glasses of water and went to the bathroom. Almost instantaneously this time, I had another positive result.

As the shock subsided, I wondered what the tablet might have done. Whether, failing to abort, I'd only made it angry. Pulling myself up, I decided to go and buy another, more expensive test.

I called Christopher as I walked back to Tesco. He was on his way to a work Christmas party.

How're you doing? he said. You got your phone back?

The warmth in his voice had such a visceral effect I looked around me on the traffic island as though he might appear there.

Did you see my email about the reunion?

Suddenly the sky lit up as if by a silent detonation.

Are you actually going?

I can't but a part of me wants to. I think you should go.

Why would I want to do that?

Morbid curiosity? You're extremely morbid.

Ha.

I want you to tell *me* about it. I'm sure you know Eddie will be there.

As I reached the petrol station, I saw that the detonation had come from a rotation of advertisements on a huge LED screen. I was disoriented and had walked the wrong way down the road.

I'd rather die.

My phone buzzed against my head. I checked the screen – an unknown number was calling – and wondered if it was my new life coach.

Isn't it too late anyway? I thought you had to sign up.

They sent round an email yesterday saying there were still places.

I haven't been reading emails.

I know. But I think you should go. His tone was mischievous.

The last time I spoke to Eddie he was *lost at sea*. Literally. Somewhere off Corsica in a sailing boat. He had a fever and I think he thought he was going to drown out there.

At the time I'd thought this meant something, but then I doubted I was the first person he'd called.

You'd be a very comforting person to speak to in that situation.

Oh?

Definitely. I feel like you'd say whatever someone wanted to hear.

The flat reeked of smoke.

Look at all the ladybirds! Mira called as I closed the door.

I came over to the window where she was standing with an ashtray. There were dozens fluttering against the glass.

Must be attracted to the light. Or maybe the glass is warm.

My skin crawled. I pointed to a figure, dimly visible below, and gave her an apprehensive look.

I don't know, she said laughing, one of the tenants? What a nuisance. Shall we call the police to our communal property? Gentrifiers here, we'd like to report a neighbour in the garden. Actually I've just been listening to some depressing thing on the radio about how they're going to review security around all public spaces because of the terrorism threat now. To stop cars running people down and make us safer, ostensibly.

I felt edgy and went round shutting blinds.

I'd choose safety over terrorism to be honest.

I know you would.

Across the street, a man came to the window just as I did. He looked down at the road, listening to a phone in one hand and holding the other to his chest.

I'm being paranoid. Forget it.

Because people are after me?

Just the feeling something's about to happen, you know that feeling.

OK, she said, now serious.

Mira's family had a dog, but a sniper shot it when it transpired dogs could anticipate a shelling.

Now her phone rang. I went to the bathroom to do the third pregnancy test but could still hear her as she answered.

Daria! Yes, of course I can speak, comrade.

I was transported. I tried to pee very quietly, waiting for her to talk, but Mira was silent for a long time. Then as her questions came – when, where, how? – I realised something was wrong. I put my head around the door, watched her face turn to me with the phone still pressed against it. Her gaze full of pity for me. I knew already what had happened and went back in again. The positive pregnancy line had appeared and my mother had died that morning.

I held the sink for balance. I thought of the photograph of us in the bath, her shoulder, and then, for a split second I thought of calling her to be comforted, before it hit me – my mother no longer existed. I couldn't call to tell her this. It was total now rather than just symbolic. We were in two separate worlds.

That night I started dreaming again for the first time since Luke broke up with me. In one I was sat at a potter's wheel, shaping with my hands a belly getting bigger and bigger until it was bigger than I could control and caved in on itself. In another, my mother was in the commune, helping me assemble mysterious items of flat-pack furniture. We gave up trying to make sense of the diagrams and made them how we thought they should look. There was one box left. She was slow dancing with it – a very tall heavy oblong. The object inside the cardboard thudded against the side as she tilted and turned, dancing toward another wall where she leant it and took it back again on the same tender journey.

In another, from which I woke finally with a jolt, a man was in bed with me, not Mira. He was bearing down and I could taste salt on his lips, feel his chest under a loose cotton shirt. At first, I thought it was Luke but then, when I found his face, I saw the man was Eddie.

In the morning I found the emails about the reunion and replied that I would be attending.

After endless fields, she recognised the cycle track now running alongside the train, the science park, sixth form college, rugby pitches and tenpin bowling, the large industrial sheds. It felt like coming up on a strong pill, the connection to these nondescript places – places she hadn't noticed when she lived there. The train window slowed alongside the station sign.

CAMBRIDGE
HOME OF ANGLIA RUSKIN UNIVERSITY

Stepping onto the platform she regretted the shoes instantly. The pair pulled from a chaos of bin bags in the half dark that morning were heeled ankle boots. She'd forgotten they were painful. Worse, it would look like she was trying to impress people.

The area around the station was completely different a decade on from her graduation. There were new buildings everywhere – mostly tech companies and luxury apartments. Still, a wave of nostalgia hit her as she went through the barriers.

As a student there she'd never felt at home, but the sensation in that moment was that this was somewhere she had used to belong and *now* did not. Estranged, as if she'd been shaped by it, like an espaliered tree trained to grow up walls, in ways that were only sensible now she was back here.

It was always colder than London. More like Glasgow. The winds swept over from Siberia in winter, someone had told her once. Too cold to walk for twenty-five minutes in these boots. As she waited for a bus, her phone buzzed with another unknown number.

The bus was taking forever so she climbed into a taxi.

She wanted to drive around but the driver refused to drive unless it was to one specific destination. Because of *the system*, he said, passengers had to travel directly.

It didn't matter. Here, Luke did not exist. Nothing was tainted by association. Here, *she* did not quite exist either, a former life that had now been overwritten.

Collecting the key to her room for the night she smiled, not recognising the man behind the desk who signed her in.

Nice to be back?

Strange.

Did he know her, or did he just know what she had come for?

Well, he grinned as if he said this a lot, the past's a foreign country.

She was out of practice making conversation with strangers.

At dinner she sat next to a civil servant who looked vaguely familiar.

I studied SPS, he said, but they don't call it that now. I can't remember what they call it.

He was working on a Balkans summit, timed for when the UK left the EU.

It's all in limbo at the moment, obviously. But it's really a hole on the map. They feel abandoned by Europe, so it's Russia they're turning to. It's how people behave when they feel excluded, they don't necessarily act rationally, as we know.

Anya nodded, taking small, dry bites of potato fondant, wondering whether he was telling her all this so arrogantly, in great detail, because he knew who she was, and blushed when he said that of course he knew.

History?

English, she said. For undergrad anyway. Didn't you roll a disco ball back from a party – he laughed – only to discover it wouldn't fit through the door? It was bike-locked outside for the rest of term as I remember.

(Was she flirting?)

That's right.

Do you have a cigarette?

Sorry, I don't.

She got up, dispirited, and walked between the long tables toward the door. The hall that had once been so intimidating now seemed tiny. The people in it too seemed small, though in that previous life they had caused Anya to feel acute self-consciousness. Such shame and resentment toward her own family.

The man's name was Kieran, she remembered. Kieran what? Oh who cared, she was not there for him.

She was becoming warm and a little woozy from the wine. She could feel her cheeks flushing, a light sheen of sweat. If Christopher had been there, they would be outside smoking together, by now doing brutal caricatures of everyone in the hall. No one was in the smoking area to give her a cigarette. Someone from the kitchen staff was vaping. They smiled at each other politely. Then Anya was suddenly ashamed. She cringed, pretending to shiver so the young man would not be offended as she turned and left. She came back inside and sat down at the end of a table. Mimed a search for something on her phone. Scrolled through a property website. Aware all the time that *he* might at any moment catch sight of her and she would not want to look like she was waiting.

The woman opposite had brought her own food. Some kind of pale pink spread for slices of dark bread that she took out of Tupperware one by one as she ate them. The spread was applied with precise strokes. Anya now remembered the woman from her corridor. The first year. A Nat Sci? Christian society, that part she knew, a gaze she'd tried to avoid. Now she caught her eye and smiled awkwardly. The woman smiled back. Maybe she didn't recognise her. Clearly she didn't care what Anya thought of her as she sat there eating her plain, self-sufficient meal.

She finished her last slice and said hello, adding, as if she was well-rehearsed in how to have these conversations, that she'd studied Chemistry. Chosen due to her wish to be an art restorer, but she had failed at that. Now she was working as a French translator, for which she discovered she had a gift while living in Paris. She was just thinking she had misjudged the woman – refusing to eat hall food was really a mark of sophistication – when she trailed off. A presence had arrived at Anya's shoulder. Without turning to look at him, she knew.

Anya never called him Eddie until after he broke up with her, but Eddie was what everyone else in their college had called him. She'd expected to feel something when she saw him and had prepared for it. Hoped for it. Something very much in existence, set under permafrost, but when reviewed afterward, back on the outside of this, safely irrelevant.

He made amusing small talk with the translator, during which he described himself as *ostensibly single*. And what about you, he said, turning to Anya.

Only after he broke up with her had she found out he'd cheated. With their mutual friend. She'd lost both of them and the wider group she'd tangentially been a part of. He had tried to blame it on his parents – a divorce from years before which he'd once boasted hadn't affected him. That was a story he liked to tell. Instead of selling up and making him – sole child from that marriage – trek back and forth between two smaller homes that might end up being very far apart, his parents took out a second mortgage and built an extension, carrying on, essentially, in the same house. That way, as Eddie would explain it, no one's life had to be disrupted unnecessarily.

He was used to being the central fact of people's lives in this way, or he found a way to put himself there if he was not already. Every story revolved around his part in it, no matter how peripheral, so Anya knew, for example, that he'd been in Paris when the Bataclan attacks had taken place. She knew because he'd marked himself as *safe*. That was, she now remembered, the last time she'd spoken to him – online at least – and not when he'd been lost off Corsica. The status updates he had composed, apparently while lying for hours on the floor of a bar, managed to include a summary of his recent professional success. He was in Paris for the Airbnb conference, the company for whom he worked. Later he was posting again, offering strangers a bed using the hashtag #opendoors.

Soon the failed restorer had moved to another table. Anya silenced another unknown number and put her phone face down. At some point during their conversation, she found herself leaning in out of habit, resting her head on his shoulder. She realised quite how drunk she was when she kissed him lightly on the cheek. She kept her head there and he'd turned toward her, but as soon as her lips touched his she recoiled. It was Luke's skin she'd been expecting. Still, she wanted to forget about death. She wanted to stop feeling, just for a moment, that she had lost everything.

Eddie had requested, and paid extra for, his same room from first year. For old times' sake, he said. Anya went back with him *to see*. Luke did not want her so this was what he'd have to accept as the logical consequence. He was driving her to do this – the most self-destructive thing she could. The idea gave her a kind of nihilistic shiver. It was better to be complicit in the destruction.

Eddie placed his hand under her skirt as she climbed the narrow stairs in front. She didn't hesitate – that was her answer. She felt sick. Vicious. Aroused. In some kind of danger. She carried on walking at the same pace, down the familiar corridor toward his room. She recalled the feeling of being that young, which was the rush of feeling adult.

They'd used to talk about the experience after it was over, like they had both just emerged from a film. He was the first person to make her come, the body who'd revealed what hers could do if she climbed on top without self-consciousness. That was what he'd meant by *animal*. She could never quite access that place now, not in the way she once had. It was too bound up with shame, or worries about the future, which animals didn't have.

She would tell herself that because she knew what was possible, and that because sometimes she could still get close, even tantalisingly so, like the parallel curve on a hairpin bend, it was the same. But it wasn't, she thought with fresh clarity as Ed put his thumb to the back of her neck and held her throat, it was not at all the same. She felt sudden grief for all the wasted time, the sacrifice she'd made for Luke's empty promise of security.

He closed the door and began taking off his shirt. As it passed over his head she saw that he was perfectly preserved. It was as if he'd been frozen cryogenically in this room, which was also just as it had been. She remembered that she hadn't shaved or waxed in months. It hardly mattered now.

The first time she met him was at a party on Mill Road. He'd been set upon by several girls after arguing that *females* only liked *guys* who posed a sexual threat. She thought of this provocation again as he pushed her forward and put her hand between her legs to show her what she knew – that she was wet already. He nudged her legs apart with his knee and wound her long hair around his fist so that her neck yanked back and it was hard to breathe. Her body locked into position. She saw it just at the edge of her vision, eyeballs straining as her head bent back toward the ceiling, all reflected in the same mirror that, aged twenty-one, he'd screwed to the inside of the door.

Ed had once whispered he would like to fuck her pregnant. He found the taut bellies and breasts of pregnant women arousing. Now she told him, the only person she would tell, and he let her neck go slack for a moment so she made eye contact with her own reflection.

The lamp beside the bed fell and smashed, glass flying everywhere. He didn't stop. All she could do was hold her breath, his teeth pulling at her ear, the shadow of him on the ceiling.

At last he let her climb over him and a dark wall of heat came down.

She woke around dawn, tongue thick, the radiator on full blast, and tried to slip out of bed but he snorted and grabbed her wrist.

Where are you off to Annie?

The old name repelled her. She hadn't been planning to leave, only to get water, but now she decided on leaving.

Don't.

He wrapped his arm around her back and pulled her down against his chest. The smell in the cave of his arm was overpowering. She looked down at their bodies – his hairy and muscled, hers covered in smears of blood. Tiny scratches. She'd forgotten the broken glass.

I really need to go.

But I *love* you! he whined in a girlish voice.

She wriggled free and started pulling on her clothes, feet bleeding now too.

Will you tell your fiancé?

Who told you?

I can't remember. But you're getting married right?

Mm hm.

Next stop, death. That'll probably be the next thing I hear about you.

Until he said that, her mother had not been dead.

It's pessimism that drives people to get married. To lock something up so it can't run off.

I see.

She pulled her boots on but they were like hot irons now. She took them off and held them in one hand.

Goodbye Ed.

Clasping the boots to her chest, she bent down, grabbed her bag and staggered through the door, down the stairs and out again into the cold. There was snow underfoot and she gasped.

For a moment she was disoriented – she knew this street, like the back of her hand, but was unable to place it on a map. The city was all made in the same stone, pretty much, seamless like a video game – no rough or discordant textures. At night it had always felt safe, if a little eerie. The homogenous unity meant walking along the empty street felt only marginally different to walking through the rooms of a house. She tipped her face to the sky and started walking, still barefoot. The street lamps seemed to be communicating with her, with each other. Communing even. She felt protected by their light and this oceanic feeling, like no harm could come to her. She walked the rest of the way as if she was being held.

On the train back to London the unknown caller became more insistent. I'd not wanted to answer because then the hope that it was Luke would be extinguished and I would instead have to have a conversation with Daria about my mother, or maybe even one of Mira's irate, book-burning Serbs who was probably hacking into her messages. I wanted to put off that moment of painful certainty, hoping it might somehow be averted. That I would wake up as if from a nightmare, the way my younger tutees ended all their stories.

When I finally answered, the caller was none of those. My aunt said she'd heard about my mother and had been trying to get hold of me. She was worried. She was herself distressed by the news. As I submitted to her gentle scolding, I found I could not contain myself any longer. I turned my face toward the window to avoid the other passengers.

She hadn't seen my mother for years but the people she knew with Alzheimer's didn't have any sense of danger, or were free of certain fears. One man near hers in Killin kept leaving his house and locking himself out, ending up in all sorts of places – the middle of the local stone circle or by a busy road. These people became a danger to themselves, yes, but they had to have their liberty. My father was right to leave her that. Even with what happened. Did I understand that? I stayed silent, not wanting to. We passed a whole field of cars tossed on top of each other like toys and it occurred to me how different things look depersonalised like that. The ball in my throat was back. Choking me. I could come and stay again, she said patiently, if I needed or wanted that. Her son Nikolaj, who went by Calum now, was working nearby and could drive me to and from the station.

The last time I stayed with her there, a house she had moved to an hour and a half north of Glasgow, was just after my first term at university. It was the first time I'd been back. Michaelmas term had ended. Drago was not yet dead. Life could now begin:

I get the train to Glasgow Central then walk from there to Queen Street. I have an hour until my next train and wander slowly to kill the time. The familiar hoppy smell makes me anxious and the pubs are full with jacked-up, warlike men. Celtic are playing Rangers. Whenever I feel intimidated by strangers on the street like that, I tell myself I'm more likely to be murdered by someone close to me. At Crianlarich, still fourteen miles from Killin, the line splits. I have to get off there and wait for Calum to get me. After Glasgow, the air is so pure and cold it hurts my lungs. There is snow on the ground and the sky throbs as if to promise more. Birds' nests sit exposed in the bare arms of trees. I pace beneath them, shivering in my charity-shop fur coat. After twenty minutes, I can't feel my hands or feet. I will learn to drive, I think, then I won't be dependent on men like him. I decide to ask Ed for lessons.

I try to picture Nikolaj. I try to remember to call him Calum. I've just spent eight weeks free of his tyranny, his face has blurred in my mind. He looks misshapen – a piece of overstuffed taxidermy. He's doing it on purpose, I know. Making me wait in this forbidding place, to establish who is powerful here. After three cars roar by I try calling him but get no answer. He has always hated me, but I'm expecting him to be merciless now I've started university. Finally his car swerves in beside me and he is grinning through the open window. Metallica, 'Fade to Black'. Happenin Oxford? He has called me this since the day I got in to Cambridge. He eyes my fur coat and sodden wheelie bag with amusement. His head's shaved and his teeth have dark rims as if he's swallowed ink. I notice, as he drives, a new tattoo. The saltire, beside the existing kilted man dragging on a spliff.

As far as I know Calum's only political views involve Scottish independence. To the extent that I live in my head and cling to cities, my cousin exults in his KGB carapace of muscle and bone, and hungers for the wild. Before coming out here to work as a ghillie he tried to be a participant on a reality show that required people to survive on an uninhabited island. He was not accepted, to my aunt's relief, but while I was revising he would watch it and sneer at the inexpert way the fud who had made the cut ahead of him now tanned animal skins or whittled spoons from logs.

He always resented his mother for leaving Yugoslavia when she did, before he was born, before he got to have that opportunity. He used to get excited at the sight of burning tanks and sparking wires, the bodies sleeping in the sun, murmuring, as we watched the news, that if he could he'd join the Tigers. The paramilitaries all had names like that. Tigers, White Eagles, Yellow Wasps. When he talked that way my aunt slapped him.

On the back seat now, I can see his rifle. We pass the falls – a white slalom against black rock – and he tells me about the big estate he works for, which has a haunted house. The wallpaper is laced with arsenic he says. But it's not the wallpaper he wants to show me. He will take me to the cottage he shares with his mother later, but first I'm to come with him. There is something immediately suspicious in the way he says this, but I know I can't refuse.

We get out by some sheds and he chucks me clothing from the boot. The dogs bark excitedly. I am strapped into Gore-tex, then he passes me a white lab coat. I ask if this is a joke. It's snowing up there, pure baltic he says, I'll need camouflage.

In the Argocat, we head up into the hills. He explains the general principles of managing the herd. Hunting deer is a matter of conservation. I have this as my frame of reference when Luke explains it to me, seven years later when we meet. I wonder if the move away from Glasgow has been good for him, a healthy outlet, or if he's just high on this new authority. He is doing real work while I'm a fandan at university.

Are you going to make me shoot a stag?

Pure gallus, Oxford. I'll shoot a hind.

Are they the women?

He rolls his eyes.

When we get to the top it is snowing heavily. In spite of the vast landscape, I feel trapped. I put the lab coat on and keep close behind, my head bowed against the wind as I follow his boots, which go quickly over the uneven terrain. Beneath the snow, the ground is either sharp rock or boggy, and every now and then I can hear the sound of water rushing away.

My eyes and nose stream. Each time we stop I look up in silence, confronted by a new scene, and wonder how I have ended up here, on the surface of another planet, with this man, in a lab coat. My lungs are in agony from running. I wonder if this is where I will die.

He points out a bird of prey and I collapse in the snow and then we are running again. My whole body is on fire except my hands and feet which are numb. Suddenly he drops down, behind a mossy verge, and I drop down beside him, relieved. He passes me a pair of binoculars – pointing out the group of hinds. They are in the distance, I know, but in the viewfinder they are right in front of me as if they have been cut out and placed there as Christmas decorations. As I'm looking, three stags dart across, only feet away, like dancers, antler arms aloft, then vanish into mist. We have to crawl up the burn, stopping every so often with the wind so they can't catch our scent.

Finally Calum holds up his hand and gives me some kind of signal, then disappears over the ridge. He is gone for a while. Inside my hood I can hear my heart beat inside my ears. I wonder if Calum counts as the kind of already-known person who might kill me, but otherwise it is peaceful, lying in the bright curve of the snow.

I return with the shot. Muffled as it was by my hood and the wind, I hear it, like a book falling flat from a shelf. I stand cautiously, stumbling toward the sound like there has been an accident. Calum is on his knees talking to it. Had a yearling, he says as I approach, we'll have to go after it in a bit. Too young to survive without a mother. Then he pulls out his knife and slits the soft belly open. The stomach must be cut out right now, he explains, and the animal bled, or the meat will spoil. The blood spills into the snow. I have never seen anything be taken apart like this. The stomach is a neat, translucent sack with a greenish tint. He slashes it open and soft, steaming grass swells from the incision, melting a patch of snow. He extracts the heart – the bullet is lodged inside. Wait here, he says. I sit beside the lifeless animal while he goes to find her young. The eyes are open but turning milky. Disembowelled, its skin looks like my coat. I stare at the entrails, splayed out on the snow, repulsed and in the same breath transfixed by them.

Beside their cottage on the estate, there is an outbuilding where he hangs the mother and then the child from hooks. He bifurcates and dismembers them in turn. I watch. He is surprisingly tender. Sliding into their flesh in a way that makes the swaying bodies open up for him like a folded-up toy – a puzzle all connected. He seems to delight in my expression, even more than the mutilation. He knows all the correct anatomical terms, and some I've never heard of. Knackery, stink pit. A stink pit, he laughs, is where dead animals are left as bait to trap more animals – foxes and other pests. He takes a cereal bar from his pocket with bloody gloves and I want to gag when he shows me pictures on his digital camera. Instead I dull my nausea with the thought of going back in a few weeks and handing in my essay on Shakespeare and the concept of authority. I will be cleansed and whole again, severing this person.

Anja? Are you still there?

She waited, listening to my breathing, then said, as she had once before, that my anger was a poison that would only end up hurting me. After she hung up I kept the phone to my ear. I clung to it first for its solidity, then as though I might break it.

When I get out at King's Cross the sky is huge. I am suspicious of the way winter is thawing, the bright blossom against pebble-dash houses. Things have come around too early.

The past keeps intruding. We are sick to death of it.

I find I am not welcome in my own home. My own country. Again and again this happens. I seem to be the common denominator. This realisation is, at first, the end of a cigarette in the dark, then a train sucking me toward it as it passes through my station. My brain is approaching the mode of concentration I know it is capable of. I focus my mind on this idea like a deeply rooted hair.

I am on the bus after my brother's suicide, not knowing I need to grieve until that moment, when I realise I can't, and I stumble off into the street where a group of men are playing saxophones. 'When the Saints Go Marching In'. It strikes me the song is not happy but apocalyptic. I am wild-eyed. I want to be in that number. Chain-smoking again. I put my hands out and watch them dance, throbbing like an electrocuted cartoon character.

Ear-splitting sounds, the kind only children and animals can make, gasping for air in the intervals until my sister slaps me across the face. We are safe, she screams, shut the fuck up.

I walk from the bus stop, a woman is walking behind me in a pair of worn-down high heels, the rubber caps need replacing. Tack, tack, tack, tack. For a moment she is the target of all my rage. It hits me what a find my notebook will make for some other passenger sitting in that aircraft. Jenny Holzer's *Lustmord* is reproduced there. I google. Right under the text, at the end of the third section, the one voiced by an observer, is an ad featuring a red raw beef patty on a grill with an ice cube in the centre, melting like a puffy nipple on the meat.

> *After seeing why he places an ice cube on his burger when grilling, I'll never make one any other way.*

> The crowd parts as my mother, held up by my father and Mira's on either side, walks away from the grave like a too-thin carnival figure. Veering into people, her cardboard head jerking, eyes rolling, her hands shaking uncontrollably as she tries to drink from a small bottle. The one she didn't send away has left.

I reach the iron gate. I look up to see if Mira has the lights on. As I walk I imagine small creatures fleeing, moving out of my way. Shuffling and hopping and diving. Luke striding through the long grass with his scythe.

I no longer feel the need to hold myself together. I am just training my gaze.

13

Something had been unfrozen through fucking. It felt like a trick, the way parts of me were coming back to life. The raw, jellied pink, the uncooked meat at the centre of things. By the time I returned to the asylum, my arms imprinted with the strap of my bag, I suspected I'd got a UTI. Mira had just left a date and called to tell me about it while I tried to pee unsuccessfully.

He's an angry man. We went for dinner and he broke a plate. Stabbed his steak knife into it ranting about Eurocrats and must have hit a weak spot. It went all over the restaurant. But it was the end of the date, at least. The other one I'm on my way to now. He's an alcoholic, I think. When we had sex last time I could smell it, in his skin. How was your reunion thing?

I could see myself in the bathroom mirror as I laughed. My eyes were all pupil. I am saying I but it feels like *we*. That will sound like I have delusions of grandeur, yet there *is* someone else now, inside me. I has dissolved. It comes and goes. It's like I'm learning a new language.

*

The next morning Mira was still not back. Her phone went straight to voicemail. I could see she was not reading my messages. I tried to push paranoid thoughts from my mind but decided not to leave the flat until she returned to it. I could barricade myself in if necessary.

At a certain point I noticed it was dark again.

My first thought when Luke calls is that he's heard about Eddie. Then maybe that he has heard about my mother. It occurs to me I wasted my time translating for him when I could have been paying attention to the last words she was saying to me.

He asks questions about what I've been up to. He's nervous. He hates speaking on the phone. I prowl around the room to leach the adrenaline from my limbs, to settle. I feel canny and sharp-clawed. I use a formal, cold tone. I control the silences, letting them go on as long as he does. I put down slow, deliberate pauses. Brief answers between his questions.

Anyway, he says at last, the main reason I'm calling – I feel myself speed up again, slow slow – they found your book and stuff. I gave them your number when they called mine, but they said you never answered.

I'm silent for a long time.

The baggage people, he prompts. The company I found online.

Still I say nothing. I have stolen his silence.

Well, I thought you'd be pleased. When they called me again I just paid the fee and confirmed my address, so I've got it. The package arrived yesterday.

I move toward the sink, wanting background noise so it will sound as if I'm busy. I boil the kettle while he continues talking, unceasing now, about logistics – ways he could now get the package to me if I tell him where I am. My hands tremble slightly. Once the kettle has boiled I pour the water away down the drain, producing a cloud of steam.

A tiny screech and smudge of brown in the corner of my vision alerts me to my victim. The mouse has somehow found its way into the sink and is now making small cries. It seems to have lost a foot thanks to the action of my kettle, dragging itself in frenzied circles.

You need to put it out of its misery, he says when I tell him. Show no mercy. Do you have a hammer or anything? Something very heavy?

I go out into the garden to fetch a brick from by the chicken coop and Luke talks me through what I need to do. I say I'm worried I'll damage the sink and he says I will have to take the risk or it's inhumane. An amputated mouse will not survive in the wild. I don't tell him that she lived with us.

We are poised to do it, me trying to control the tremor in my hand, Luke coaxing me, but when I bring the brick down, his gentle encouragement in my ear, I feel faint. His tenderness makes me hesitate at the last moment, so that instead of dashing the mouse's brains out before it can feel more pain, I torture her with a slow, medieval death, slowly pressing into the softness of her body until there's a snap and then a crunch, like a plastic cup under a wheel.

I have tried to go back and explain who I was in those last moments, and what I return to is the mouse, the brick and that sound.

I try to explain that I felt my own power, godlike, and as I did, the way I saw things changed. I look at the head of a small dog now, and know that I could crush it. My chest felt cold but no longer tight as if something had unzipped it.

I gave Luke my new address and said that he could either post it or, if getting to the post office was too much trouble, drive it round to me that night.

Stay there, he said, as I knew he would, I'll come to you. Forty minutes. Forty-five.

Darkness presses in at the windows. Mira's still not back. I take my washbag to the bathroom and place it on the swirling linoleum before taking out a razor and tweezers. I stand before the mirror, serene and just visibly pregnant. I think of internal rupturing. The idea makes me giddy. I run the hot tap and hold the razor to my arm. Pause. If I start at my knuckles, why not drag the blade over every inch of me? I replace the razor and put my hand against my swollen stomach.

I notice a hangnail and as I pull, skin comes with it. At the sight of the pinkness, my mouth begins to water. I must be craving iron. The finger pulses and yes – I am craving meat.

Mira has a whole chorizo in the fridge. I take it, crouching on my haunches.

I can see the man at his window again, watching me eat, stark naked. I slide the mouse into the bin, still warm like a discarded teabag.

There is the swaying noise of a car alarm outside. Either it has just started or I have only just noticed it. Louder then quieter in waves but never ceasing. I try to decide whether it is really outside my head or only inside. It sounds almost like cicadas.

I start rifling for the box I know has souvenirs. All the mementos I kept from the early days. Venetian saints. I find the programme for the Olympics opening ceremony, *Isles of Wonder*, the intro by Danny Boyle.

I lie in wait with the brick beside the bed, imagining the scene, the road locked down, trembling cordons and blue lights glimmering. I take a picture, turning my phone's camera, staring directly into the eye of its black lens.

When Luke arrives at the front door I wait to buzz him in, then lope a few more times around the room to let off steam. I visualise smoothing fresh tarmac over everything, filling every crack, every flaw I have been picking at obsessively for years. The way is clear and new again.

I smell him in the hall before I see him.

The nowness of him in fisheye, the specificity, caught in my throat. This time I did not see a stranger. I saw exactly who he was. When he entered everything about him seemed enlarged. Certain. He gleamed and bulged. His pores, the shine of his teeth, the flakes inside his ears all magnified. He told me that I looked different though, his eyes sliding over my new frame as if afraid.

He is careful not to come too near. I'm a floating terror to him now. Shyly, he puts down the package and picks up the brick, inspects it with a frown, then wraps it in kitchen roll. Then, as if we haven't just spoken on the phone, he repeats most of what he's already said to me. I tell him I've started running. I've been learning how to drive.

It is inspired, what happens next.

Do you want to see me driving?

He is eyeing the bed in the centre of the room. When's Mira coming back?

Too soon. Let's go for a drive.

Anya wouldn't use that tone. He looks at me but I am deadly serious.

Aren't you going to open it? He nudges the package toward me.

I shake my head as if there's something I need more urgently and he takes my hand, kneading my fingers.

I guess you can drive me down your road, I'd like that. Then would you come back with me?

As the car slides forward, I feel everything go quiet. The past disappears and so does the future. I have only the present tense. My ears grow alert, my sense of smell so keen I can hold and separate every element inside the car. The leather seats, his sweat, his hair. The silence was like music. I keep my eyes on the road, moving very slowly in the direction of the station.

The car is automatic. Driving is easier than I expected.

I've had dreams in which I was put in charge of a car without knowing how to drive it, and those were horrifying and exhausting, but this! It feels like when I first broke into a run. I'll have to rethink what I'm capable of. What other things might come naturally to me.

I turn to him then again and, as when he'd come through the doorway, it is as if I am seeing him for the first time clearly, except that it feels final now, and when I turn back to the road what I see feels as good as an end.

The road stretches on and on. The buildings either side a blur like the edge of a black hole. No place to turn. Level and straight and stretching resolutely nowhere. I put my hand behind my passenger's head, warm, feeling the weight of his skull. I should have liked to have kept it.

I press my foot down on the accelerator. I do not see the curb. For a long time it is as if we have lifted off the road and are flying. My passenger, now my captive, holds on to the door. Shouting. Let me out, he repeats, let me out! As if I've lost control instead of taken it. Stop the car. Anya, fucking hell! Please, I beg you, stop. The longer I stay silent and the car careers on, the more it seems I can do this, just as he said. Faintly I hear him now. I press my foot down harder.

ACKNOWLEDGEMENTS

This book is dedicated to my grandparents and dispersed Balkan family past and present – from Montenegro to Mexico, Serbia to Scotland, Arizona to Acton. I made a tentative start on AR at the end of 2015, so it exists thanks to many people, conversations and acts of kindness over five years in which the world has changed significantly. It is a work of fiction, but one which draws on a sensitive history and painful reality for many. I'm indebted to the people I met in Bosnia, particularly Jasminko Halilović and the work of the War Childhood Museum. I'm also grateful for conversations with Vesna Petković, Ana Baric, Tamara Platiša, Svetlana Rakočević, Vesna Goldsworthy, Ana Russell-Omaljev, Maria Ratković Vidaković and Vladimir Unkovski-Korica, as well as the audiences at the Southeast European Future Festival and Serbian Literary Festival in London. I count my lucky stars for Emma Paterson and Angelique Tran Van Sang – thank you both for your transformative help. Thank you also to Saba Ahmed for her invaluable copyedit, Greg Heinimann for the cover, Lauren Whybrow for prising it out of my hands, and everyone at Bloomsbury and Aitken Alexander. In Brussels, thanks to Piet Joostens and Passa Porta who gave me the time, space and stipend to begin writing in earnest. Thanks to Thea Seger who read the first pages and alleviated second novel syndrome enough to keep going. Thanks to the supportive community of writers, readers and booksellers I've met online, I won't list you but I'm glad *Sympathy* did not deter you from making contact with an author via Instagram. Thank you to my friends and apologies for any fictionalised anecdotes you may find, also to my cousin who has the kilt/spliff tattoo. Thank you to my parents, uncle Branislav, and ONS, again.